Thirteen is bad luck?

As Darci headed toward a row of cabins, she noticed a small wooden building — marked CAMP OFFICE. A row of silver cups gleamed in the window. Darci walked over to take a look. Above the row of cups hung a little sign saying the trophies were for the girls in the cabin that contributed the most to Pine Tree Camp. Darci stared at the silver cups. What would it be like to go home with one of those?

Darci suddenly realized another girl had come up alongside her. "Aren't those silver cups fabulous?" Darci exclaimed, adding, only half-kidding, "I sure hope my cabin will win them."

"You might as well forget it," the girl said loftily. "We're in Cabin 10, and on a scale of one to ten — you know you can't beat that." She looked smug. "What cabin are you in?"

"13," Darci answered.

The girl smirked. "You see?" she said. "Thirteen is bad luck."

Darci in Cabin 13

Martha Tolles

AN
APPLE
PAPERBACK

SCHOLASTIC INC.
New York Toronto London Auckland Sydney

ISBN 0-590-41917-X

12 11 10 9 8 7 6 5 4 3 2 1   9/8 0 1 2 3 4/9

Printed in the U.S.A.   28
First Scholastic printing, June 1989

To Roy, my favorite camper

Contents

1. Smash-up

Darci Daniels clutched her big shoulder bag, her tennis racket, two paperback books, and her backpack, which stuck up in front of her face as she jumped off the camp bus. But instead of landing on her feet in the parking lot of Pine Tree Camp, she crashed wham, smack, into somebody.

"Uh-h-h!" she exclaimed.

"O-oof!" the other person grunted, and they went tumbling down onto the ground together. Darci's sunglasses flew off her face, and everything spilled out of her arms. And she found herself sitting on the ground, surrounded by the legs and feet of the other campers and staring right into the face of a blond boy.

"What *happened*?" Darci said as she struggled to her feet. "I didn't mean to crash into you like that."

"It was just an accident, huh?" a voice spoke

1

sarcastically from behind them. Darci looked around to see a tall, dark-haired girl glaring at her.

But before she could speak, the boy said, "Here, I'll help you pick up your stuff."

"Oh. Oh, thanks." Darci flashed him a smile. He was cute, blond hair, blue eyes, and older, too. What fun to go to a camp right next to one for boys!

She bent and began to gather up all her belongings that had fallen out of her shoulder bag — hair brush, postcards, address book, cherry lip gloss, even her wallet, which was lying open to a picture of her parents and two brothers.

But the blond boy was peering at the two paperbacks she had dropped.

Embarrassed, she reached for them. But too late. He'd picked them up. Darci felt herself growing hot in the face. The books, *Love for Laurie* and *Romance for Marie*, had been given to her by a friend to read on the trip. She had another book — a *serious* book about birds — in her duffel, but how could she explain that now?

"Say, you'll really need these," the boy said, handing her the books with a grin.

"*Ha,*" the tall girl scoffed loudly, tossing back her thick, dark hair. "Some crazy reading, huh,

Greg?" The girl had long, sparkly earrings that swung in her ears, and she looked at Greg as if she knew him. Darci wished she knew him, too. But she wasn't so sure about the girl. She didn't seem very friendly.

"Thanks for helping me," she said to Greg. The girl hadn't bothered to help, Darci noticed.

Just then a voice called out from the crowd around the bus, "Darci Daniels, Cabin 13." It was Mrs. Burkett, the camp director.

"I guess I better go," Darci said.

"Good-bye, Darci." Greg smiled at her.

She smiled back. "See you." She hoped she would! The dark-haired girl didn't say anything.

Spotting her duffel bag in the growing mound of luggage, Darci grabbed it with her free hand. Now she must find Cabin 13. She set off across the parking lot, jammed with buses and cars, and boys, who would be at Birch Camp, and girls, who would be at Pine Tree Camp.

Darci followed a crowd of girls as they crossed a clearing in front of a large, brown wooden building. Everywhere she looked were tall, green pines, and off to the left was the blue circle of Pine Lake. The water looked cool and smooth and rippled gently against a sandy beach, where a cluster of green boats were tied to a dock. Darci drew in a breath of piney New Hampshire air. She was glad that her mom and dad had suggested she come to camp, especially since they'd had no special vacation plans. Her older brother was working, her younger brother going to day camp. It had seemed like a perfect time for Darci to go away to camp.

As Darci headed toward a row of cabins, she noticed a small wooden building marked CAMP OFFICE. A row of silver cups gleamed in the window. Darci walked over to take a look. Above the row of cups hung a little sign saying the trophies were for the girls in the cabin that contributed the most to Pine Tree Camp. Darci stared at the silver cups. What would it be like to go home with one of those? Her older brother had a whole row of cups he'd won in baseball and soccer, and her mom and dad had some from tennis matches they'd won. Wouldn't her family be amazed and impressed if she walked in with a trophy of her own?

Darci suddenly realized another girl had come up alongside her. "Aren't those silver cups fabulous?" Darci exclaimed, adding, only half-kidding, "I sure hope my cabin will win them."

"No way," the girl said scornfully. She was a heavy-set girl with a square, determined-looking chin. "Our cabin's in line for them this year. My friend Bettina has been planning it ever since last summer. Everyone in *our* cabin has been coming to this camp for years."

"You mean it's already decided who's going to win before camp's even begun?" Darci was taken aback. "That doesn't seem right." How could they know already? And what difference did it make if these girls had come here other summers?

"You might as well forget it," the girl said loftily. "We're all in Cabin 10, and on a scale of one to ten — you know you can't beat that." She looked smug. "What cabin are you in?"

"Thirteen," Darci answered.

The girl smirked. "You see?" she said. "Thirteen is bad luck."

"I don't think so," Darci said firmly. "My father was born on the thirteenth."

The girl just shrugged. "Well, I have to go now to find my friends." She held up her arm displaying a bracelet made of narrow, brown strips of leather braided together. "We all wear these friendship bracelets. We made them years ago when we first started coming to Pine Tree Camp together."

With that, the girl left, leaving Darci to walk on by herself.

At last Darci found Cabin 13. A girl with curly black hair stood on the steps, looking around.

"Hi," Darci called out. "Do you live here?"

"Sure do." The girl grinned at her. Huge, red earrings swung in her ears, and she wore a large, loose top over skin-tight pants. She also had on heavy eye makeup. Darci thought the girl looked terrific. "Are you Darci?" the girl asked.

"Yes." Darci stopped before the smiling girl, getting good, friendly vibes so far.

"My name's Ashley," the girl said enthusiastically. "I was here last summer, too."

Darci's heart sank. What if Ashley was as snobby as the girls in Cabin 10? Quickly, Darci looked at Ashley's arms. Good. At least she wasn't wearing a friendship bracelet.

Just then Darci heard some screams. She turned to see a pack of girls racing past, all talking and laughing and yelling, and at the head of the pack was that tall, dark-haired girl she'd met earlier in the parking lot with Greg.

"Who are they?" Darci said to Ashley. But somehow she knew the answer, and it wasn't one that gave her good vibes. As she watched them go running on up the path, she realized that one of the girls was the same one who had told her about the trophies.

Ashley frowned. "They're the girls in Cabin 10. They've been coming to this camp for years and years and they think it makes them better than

6

everyone else!" Ashley's frown suddenly changed to a smile. "Maybe we'll show 'em, right?" she said to Darci.

"Right," Darci agreed, feeling pleased. This girl, even if she had been here last year, seemed friendly. Darci turned to the cabin door. "I guess I better take my stuff in and start unpacking. I wonder which bunk I should use and all that."

"I'll show you," Ashley offered, and she led the way into the cabin.

Darci followed her into the small cabin with its brown wooden walls and wooden floor. She saw there were five bunks, three on one wall, two on the other, with a footlocker at the end of each one. There was also a small mirror and a shelf by each bed. It was a lot different from having a whole bedroom to yourself, Darci thought. Still, it looked kind of cozy.

"Our cabin leader is at a meeting right now. She'll sleep here." Ashley pointed to the bunk by the door. "I'm in that corner bunk. Why don't you take the one right across from me? Our other two cabinmates haven't come yet. They're new, too."

Darci was glad to hear that. Maybe new girls would be easier to get to know than old ones.

She walked over to the corner bunk and dropped her shoulder bag and duffel and tennis racket on the floor. On her bunk was a stack of sheets and green blankets and a pillow. "I guess I ought to start to unpack then."

"Sure," Ashley said. "I've already put my stuff away."

So Darci opened her duffel, and there right on top was a picture of her family. She lifted it out and put it on her shelf by her mirror.

"Let's see your family." Ashley came over to look at it. In the picture Darci's mom and dad and two brothers were standing on the front step of their house. They seemed so far away. It made Darci a little sad to think she wouldn't be seeing them for a whole month.

"He's cute. He's a real hunk." Ashley pointed to Darci's older brother.

"Really? You think so?" Darci had to laugh. Her tall, skinny brother was a hunk? Just then she glanced up in the mirror at the two of them, Ashley with her dark mop of hair and heavy eye makeup and Darci, brown-eyed with curly brown hair. Their reflections were both smiling and they had friendly expressions on their faces. That gave Darci a good feeling.

"What grade are you in?" Darci asked.

"Going into seventh." Ashley rolled her eyes happily. "Junior high. I can't wait."

"Me, too," Darci exclaimed. "I'll be starting seventh, too."

"Great. We're just the same, aren't we? Can I help you unpack?" Ashley asked.

"Sure. Thanks." And looking at this smiling girl, Darci felt that maybe she had one friend at Pine Tree Camp already.

2. Surprise

Supper in the Mess Hall on Darci's first night at Pine Tree Camp was like eating in the school cafeteria, but at the wrong time of day. And the whole room was filled with unfamiliar faces. Darci suddenly felt very far away from home. Even though they were having pizza and fruit, both favorites of hers, she wasn't as hungry as she'd thought she'd be.

But she liked sitting with Ashley and the other two girls from her cabin. Julie had shiny, straight, dark hair and braces on her teeth. Sara wore glasses and lived in New York City, she told them.

The Cabin 10 girls, including the tall, dark-haired one who turned out to be the one named Bettina, also sat at Darci's table. For the first few days, they sat at assigned tables. After that they could sit wherever they wanted. Good, thought Darci, as she listened to the Cabin 10 girls bragging and bragging about everything they'd done at Pine Tree Camp. They were all wearing their leather friendship bracelets, Darci noticed.

"Have you ever been to camp before?" Bettina called down the long table to Darci.

Darci shook her head. "I've been camping with my family a lot."

Bettina smiled smugly at her friends, Fran, a chubby girl with a square chin, Fran's twin, Lana, who was very thin and didn't look like her sister at all, and a girl with a shaggy haircut named Gillian. "That's not exactly the same, going with your parents." Bettina sounded scornful.

"That's right," Fran added quickly. "Bettina's been coming here for years, all of us have. We're used to being on our own."

"My mother came to this camp when she was a girl, too," Bettina continued. "I really know *all* about the place." Bettina had dark eyelashes and green eyes. Darci thought, she's a really nice-looking girl. Too bad she doesn't act nice!

But before Darci could answer, Mrs. Burkett stood up and rapped on her water glass for quiet. She was an athletic-looking woman wearing green shorts and a white shirt. "Welcome, girls, to Pine Tree Camp," she began. Darci was glad she didn't have to talk anymore to Bettina right now. She'd rather hear about all the things they were going to be doing at camp.

Mrs. Burkett continued, "I know you'll enjoy our program here. We'll be having tennis, swimming, volleyball, and softball. And there'll be nature walks, crafts, and a few activities with the boys at Birch Camp: a movie, for instance."

"There're some cute boys at Birch," Ashley whispered to Darci.

Darci nodded. She knew. She would enjoy the movie, no matter what it was, if she got to see Greg.

"And this year," Mrs. Burkett went on, "we have added something new. I'm not going to tell you about it now. It's a surprise for you, and we're going to begin it tomorrow."

Several kids waved their hands in the air. "What is it, Mrs. Burkett?"

Mrs. Burkett laughed. "No, I can't tell you. We'll just keep it a secret. But tomorrow we'd like the older girls to be ready at three o'clock. I'm going to ask all of you to have your bathing suits on and meet down by the dock." Then Mrs. Burkett introduced the cabin leaders and the counselors, who were sitting at her table. And by that time everyone had finished supper.

With that Mrs. Burkett dismissed all the campers from the dining hall. Everybody was buzzing about this news, but no one could figure it out.

Darci felt a little thrill of excitement. Camp was definitely going to be okay.

When they got back to their cabin, the newcomers, Sara and Julie, began to unpack their clothes. It seemed sort of friendly, just the four of them.

"Would you like any help?" Darci asked, remembering how much she'd liked it when Ashley offered to help her.

Both Sara and Julie said yes.

"I've got so much stuff here," Sara said. "I brought a lot of drawing paper and paints with me. I was really happy to hear Mrs. Burkett say there'll be crafts every day."

"And plenty of sports, too," Julie said enthusiastically. She took a pile of green-and-white camp clothes and dropped them into her foot locker. "Do the rest of you mind being in a cabin with the number thirteen? That girl Fran kept telling me at supper it was bad luck."

"Don't listen to her," Ashley scoffed. "There's always been a Cabin 13 here. That's just superstition."

"It could mean good luck," Darci said. "My dad was born on the thirteenth."

"What I want to know is," Sara said, "what's the surprise?"

"I haven't a clue," Ashley grinned at them and shook her red earrings. "I wish it was the movie with the guys. Or gymnastics. I really like that a lot."

"Do you, Ashley?" Darci was impressed.

"Here's a picture of me." Ashley went to her locker and pulled out a snapshot of herself dressed in gymnastic clothes.

After they'd admired Ashley's picture, they looked at one of Julie with her three brothers, and one of Sara with her parents. "I think I'll like camp because there'll be so many kids to do things with. I won't be lonesome," Sara said, her eyes shining behind her glasses.

"That's right," Ashley assured her. "You're never alone for a minute here." She turned to her bunk. "But right now I think we ought to make up our beds."

They were all busily putting the sheets and blankets on their beds, when suddenly the cabin door opened, and in came a tall, red-haired teen-ager. She looked to be about seventeen, Darci thought.

"Hi, kids. I'm your cabin leader, Gail. Sorry I couldn't get here sooner, but Mrs. Burkett wanted to talk to us again after supper. But I see you're doing all right, getting all settled." She looked approvingly at the four girls, their bunks almost made and their unpacking finished.

Darci exchanged looks with her cabinmates. They might be the new girls at camp, but they were still doing just fine.

"Gail," Darci said, "can you tell us anything about tomorrow? Just what we do and all that?"

"Yeah. What's the big surprise?" Ashley asked. "Maybe they're going to start a gymnastics program. Or are we going to visit the guys?"

"Afraid not." Gail laughed. "But it's something just as good." She sat down on her footlocker. "Anyway, this is the program for tomorrow: tennis and swimming in the morning, that's after cleaning up the cabin. Then lunch, a rest time, crafts or volleyball, and at three is the surprise."

Darci wondered how she could bring up the subject of the silver cups. "I saw some trophies. . . ." she began.

Gail grinned. "I'm glad you brought that up, Darci. Everybody has a chance at winning, and I sure hope you guys are interested. I'd love to have a winning cabin."

"What do you have to do to win?" Darci asked.

"Well, you should be a good citizen, participate to the best of your ability in all the sports and activities, help others, keep a tidy cabin, make

Pine Tree Camp a good place to come to."

They all groaned and Ashley joked, "Oh, easy. Nothing to it."

But of course that wasn't so at all. It would be hard to do all those things and be that great. That night when Darci got in bed, she couldn't stop thinking about it. She hardly noticed her narrow bunk and the scratchy camp blanket, hardly had time to feel homesick. Worries tumbled through her mind. Would her tennis game be good enough for Pine Tree Camp? Could she improve her forehand? And what was the surprise for tomorrow? Would she be able to do it, whatever it was? Above all, was there any chance her cabin might win the trophies?

3. Show-off!

The next day started off fine. Sunlight was streaming through the cabin windows and birds were twittering outside in the green pines.

After breakfast Darci and her cabinmates went to their first session of tennis. The counselor, Babs, let Darci and Ashley be partners, and they played doubles with two other girls and managed to beat them. Afterwards as they walked back to their cabin, Ashley said, "You have a great backhand."

"And you're good at the net," Darci said, pleased. "We make a terrific team."

"Oh, Darci, I think so, too." And they grinned at each other. I hope we get to be good friends, Darci thought happily.

Then, when it was time for swimming in Pine Tree Lake, the counselor named Babs had them all swim back and forth while she checked their strokes and breathing. Darci thought she did pretty well. After that they had a free-swim period and Babs called out, "Now you can do whatever you like, but choose a partner, please."

Darci looked quickly at Ashley and to her pleasure, Ashley waved and nodded back at her. Their cabinmates, Julie and Sara, chose each other for partners, too, and the four of them had a great time, splashing around and diving down deep, deep into the cool water.

But at lunch Darci and her cabinmates had to sit with Bettina and her friends again. Listening to them talk about how good their tennis had been that morning, Darci knew she'd be glad when she and her cabinmates could sit with some of the other girls.

Bettina began to talk about the surprise for that afternoon. "I'll bet it's not that big a deal," Bettina said loftily. "I know pretty well what happens around here."

Darci felt annoyed by her superior attitude. "Do they have a lot of surprises at camp, then?" Darci asked pointedly.

"Well, not exactly," Bettina admitted.

"Then it could be anything," Ashley put in.

"Yeah," agreed Sara. "Maybe it's something great."

Everyone began talking at once, but Bettina flashed Darci an angry look. Uh-oh, thought

Darci. Bettina didn't like my arguing with her about the surprise.

That afternoon, dressed in their bathing suits, the girls followed Babs down to the lake.

"What is it? What's the surprise?" they kept asking, but Babs wouldn't tell them.

"Just wait. You'll see any minute now." Babs peered up the lake, and a moment later a motorboat came speeding along from the direction of the boys' camp. The counselor nicknamed Princess was driving it. She was very regal and wore her hair in a long, dark braid down her back, and everyone said she looked like an Indian princess.

Darci felt a surge of excitement. "I think I know what the surprise is," she whispered to Ashley.

And then Babs called out, "Okay, kids, now we'll do some waterskiing!"

Some of the girls cheered, and Darci was one of them. "Terrific!" she exclaimed to her friends. She'd done waterskiing lots of times on camping trips to a river with her family.

"Darci, do you know how?" asked Julie.

"That's great," said Ashley.

"Who wants to go first?" Babs yelled.

"I will," Darci called out eagerly.

Babs looked pleased. "Okay, Darci! Come on up here."

Darci hurried forward past the other girls, and

in a moment she'd donned a life jacket and jumped into the water. Babs slid some skis through the water toward her, and Darci began to ease her feet into the bindings.

"Do they fit okay?" Babs asked. "Do you know how?"

Darci nodded confidently. "Sure," she said. Princess revved up the motor, and Babs climbed into the seat beside her and threw Darci a ski rope.

Darci glanced back at the shore for one second where all the girls were lined up to watch. What had she done? She'd volunteered to put on a demonstration in front of the whole camp. She'd better be good. She just hoped she wasn't out of practice. After all, she hadn't done this since the summer before.

"Ready?" Babs called over the motor. "Just shout out 'Hit it' when you're ready to go."

Darci nodded and held on tightly to the handle of the rope as the boat towed her slowly forward. She tried to remember the things her mom and dad and her older brother had taught her. "Lean back. Don't try to stand up too soon," they always said. She gripped the handle. Don't make a mess of it, she warned herself. She was ready.

"Hit it!" she called out.

The boat started forward, tightening the ski rope. She kept her knees bent and gradually let the boat pull her up out of the water till she was standing up straight. Now the boat was pulling her along, and she was skiing behind it. And oh, it felt so good, like flying over the glassy-smooth water, the wind blowing into her hair and eyes. She swayed a little to one side and cut off to the left, and cold spray blew all over her.

It was fantastic, like being a large bird, flying over the water, going back and forth, swinging from side to side behind the boat. "Yippe-e-e," she shouted into the air with delight and wished they'd go past the boys' camp, wished that Greg could see her. But now the boat was turning to come back to the beach, and she swung in a wide arc out behind it, white spray flying high beside her. Oh, it was fun, fun. And as they drove closer to the beach, Darci tossed away the rope and sank gracefully into the water, waving to the girls as she did so.

A cheer went up from shore, and Darci grinned. Never in her wildest thoughts had she expected to be putting on a show on her second day of camp. The girls actually clapped for her as she pulled off the skis and came up out of the water.

"Thanks. Thanks!" She laughed, shaking her

wet hair out of her eyes as she hurried toward her cabinmates.

But as she passed Bettina, Bettina looked at her scornfully. And moving close to Darci, she said in a low voice, "What a show-off. What an absolute, conceited show-off!"

4. Makeup

Bettina's words kept coming back to Darci. For the next few days, even while she was rushing from games to swimming to crafts to meals and to bed again, she couldn't forget about what Bettina had said.

"Ashley," she said one day, "when we had waterskiing the other day, did you think I, uh, was showing off?" It hurt to say it.

But to her relief Ashley just grinned. "No way, Darci! You made our cabin look good. Would you help me learn how when we have our next ski?"

"Of course. I'd love to." Darci was pleased to be asked, and Ashley's praise erased Bettina's ugly words.

But that afternoon something else happened when Darci was out in the shower house. She'd been one of the last to get a turn, and she took her time in the shower, letting the prickly needles of hot water fall all over her. It was quiet, too, and peaceful with everyone else gone.

Suddenly Darci heard the door open and the voices of some girls as they came in. She wasn't paying much attention at first as she let the warm water stream over her. But then she caught a few words, something about waterskiing, and she heard a voice say, "You know what? I think they're trying to beat us out of the silver cups."

The other girl laughed loudly. "They don't have a chance, no way."

"And now they think they've got just the *best* water-skier that ever lived, and she'll try to teach her cabinmates, too," the first girl went on. "What a complete show-off she is!"

Bettina and Fran! And they must be talking about her. Darci's face began to burn with embarrassment.

She poked her head out of the shower. Through the steamy air in the room she could see their startled faces. "I was *not* showing off," she said loudly. "I was just trying to do my best, that's all. And my friends *want* to learn to water-ski! Can't you understand that?"

Bettina and Fran stared for a second, burst into laughter, then whirled around and rushed out of the shower room. Darci could hear their giggles floating back as they went through the door. Those girls! Darci turned off the shower and hurried into her clothes. The nerve of them!

When she got back to the cabin she was glad to find Ashley there.

"Ashley," she exclaimed, "listen to what just happened to me."

When she finished Ashley scowled. "What's wrong with them? I hope you told those Cabin 10 creeps they had no business saying all that."

"Well, I tried," Darci answered. "But it was so unfair of them. It's not my fault I know how to water-ski!"

"It's because Bettina's always boasting about how good they are at things. That's one thing she can't brag about," Ashley said. She gave Darci a wink. "Maybe there are other things we are better at, too. Maybe we *will* win the silver cups." She grinned, and Darci grinned back, glad she had Ashley for a new friend.

After talking to Ashley, Darci didn't mind what Bettina had said so much. She threw herself into all the tennis matches and swimming and volley-ball. She was doing well, too, and so were Ashley, Sara, and Julie. Their cabin leader noticed it.

"You guys are great," Gail said. "There's Darci, our star on the water skis. And Sara's creating a terrific poster over in crafts. Julie is just plain good at sports, Ashley's a tennis ace, and you're all doing a good job cleaning up the cabin, too."

"Wish they had gymnastics here," Ashley said longingly. "I could really *ace* that."

"I know. It'd be nice. But at least we've added waterskiing twice a week." Gail looked at them with obvious approval, and it made Darci feel good.

But one day it rained all day. Darci and her cabinmates wrote letters home, read their books, played games, but still it rained. Darci finally went to the window and stared out at the wet, green pines and cloudy skies. Still another hour until supper!

Suddenly the door opened, and Gail came in with water dripping off her raincoat. "Guess what, kids?" She shook out her red hair. "I've got great news for you. Mrs. Burkett has decided to show the movie tonight in the Mess Hall, and the boys are invited, too."

"Tonight?" Darci echoed. Immediately the thought shot through her mind — would she see Greg? She still remembered just what he looked like, though she hadn't seen him since that first day.

"Fantastic," Ashley beamed. "I'm going to start getting ready right now."

"Oh, Ashley," Julie scoffed. "You've got a whole hour yet before supper. What in the world is there to do?"

Ashley rushed over to her footlocker and pulled out a red cosmetic bag. "Are you kidding? I've got to get busy. This takes time." She emptied out a whole pile of cosmetics on her bunk.

"See, I've got peach gloss, plum blush, midnight mascara," she said as she spread out the bottles and tubes of makeup.

"But it'll be dark in the movie," Julie protested.

Ashley just shrugged and began to spread cream all over her face. "Want to try some, you guys?"

"It'd be a waste for me with all this metal on my teeth." Julie rubbed her finger over her braces, then picked up a tennis ball and tossed it to Sara. "Let's play catch."

But Darci was watching Ashley as she spread the cream on her face. True, the Mess Hall would be dark during the movie, but the lights would be on before and afterwards.

Ashley peered in her mirror on the wall and spread great quantities of tan liquid all over her face. She grinned at Darci in the mirror. "Why don't you try some of my makeup?" she urged.

Darci decided it would be a great idea. All she had with her was lip gloss. And what if she did have a chance to see Greg tonight? She would look especially good with all that glamorous makeup on her face.

"Oh, Ashley, would you let me? You wouldn't mind sharing?"

"No, no. You're my friend, aren't you?"

"Of course," Darci agreed happily.

"Let me know if you two need any help," Gail said, looking amused. She stretched out on one of the bunks with a pad and pencil.

"I know all about cosmetics," Ashley said airily. "Come on, Darci. Why don't you start with this foundation? It'll be perfect on you."

In a moment Darci's face was covered with tan liquid. And then Ashley dabbed pink blusher on her own cheeks and let Darci do the same. Next Ashley put on eyeliner. Then lots of dark mascara on her lashes, so her eyes really stood out. They looked almost like the eyes of a deer, really good, Darci thought.

"Looks great," Darci said admiringly. She began to do it, too. And how different she looked! "Terrific," she said, standing back staring at herself. "I hardly look like me at all." Her cheeks glowed, and her brown eyes looked big and dark and years and years older. What would Greg think if he saw her? Would he even know her?

All through supper she found it hard to chew or laugh or talk or anything because she was so afraid of ruining her makeup. But it was worth it, of course. "You look terrific," she kept telling Ashley.

"You both do," Sara, sitting across from them, said. "I almost wish I'd tried it."

"Yeah, you look good," a girl next to Sara added. "Your eye shadow is nice and dark."

Darci and Ashley looked at each other with satisfaction.

As supper went along, Darci discovered the Cabin 10 girls sitting at the table right behind hers. She'd been dimly aware of a lot of loud laughing and talking. Now she wondered what was so funny. Then she realized they were talking about boys over at Birch Camp.

A moment later she heard Bettina saying, "Sure, there're a lot of nice guys over at Birch Camp. And there's one who is so-o-o cute." There was another outburst of giggling.

Darci poked Ashley just as Fran said, "We can guess who that is. It's Greg, isn't it, Bettina?" There was more muffled laughter.

Darci heard that with a sinking heart. "Ashley, did you hear them?" she whispered.

Ashley nodded. "Yes, and I know who Greg is. He was here last summer, too. I think Bettina likes him."

"That's bad news," Darci groaned.

"Why, Darci?" Ashley bent toward her. "What's up? Do you know him?"

Darci whispered back. "I bumped into him the first day of camp, that's all. I was just hoping to get to know him."

Ashley made a sad face. "That's too bad, Darci."

Now supper was ending, and in a minute, the boys from Birch Camp came crowding into the Mess Hall. Darci scanned the crowd eagerly, trying to spot Greg. "Look, I see him," she whispered to Ashley.

Just as she said that, she saw Bettina jump out of her seat and rush over to the side of the hall and start talking to him.

A few others had gotten up, too, but Mrs. Burkett rose from her seat and called out, "Will the boys please sit down in the empty chairs at the back of the room? Everyone else go back to your places. And now, let's have it dark, please."

The lights blinked out, and it was time for the movie. Darci wondered if she'd get a chance to speak to Greg. What bad luck that Bettina liked him, too!

5. Secret Note

When the lights went on after the movie, Darci blinked her eyes stickily and almost rubbed them. Then she remembered why they felt so strange. It was the mascara. She quickly looked toward the back of the Mess Hall and spotted Greg. "I see him," she whispered to Ashley. Everyone was standing up now, pushing back chairs, talking loudly about the movie, a funny one about a boy who went back in time.

"Oh, I see a boy I used to know last summer," Ashley said excitedly. "His name's Rolf. Let's go talk to him. Come on, Darci."

Ashley rushed off through the crowd, knocking into people and saying, "Oops, sorry, sorry."

Darci decided to follow her. Why not? So what if Bettina did know Greg? Darci eased through the crowd and then hung around in the aisle between the chairs. Greg was coming her way. He'd have to pass her, have to see her. And, oh, was she glad she had worn all this makeup!

"Hi," she called out as he approached.

"Well, hi-i-i." He stopped in front of her with a little surprised look on his face. Then he smiled at her. "Say, you're looking good tonight. Different, too."

He must have noticed her makeup! "Well, I promise not to crash into you again."

"Oh, yeah, yeah." He laughed and ducked behind his arms, pretending to shield himself. He had nice, tanned arms. "I forgot," he added. "You could be dangerous. So how're you doing? Have you been reading much?" He grinned a little. He was remembering her paperbacks, she thought. Those silly romantic ones. Was that why he was laughing at her?

"I've been reading my bird book," she said quickly. She'd impress him with that anyway. "It has some great photographs in it, too." She wondered if Bettina would think of better things to talk about. Then she thought of something really good herself. "We had a lot of fun waterskiing the other day," she added.

His blue eyes lit up. "Yeah, we did, too. Do you know how?"

"Oh yes, I do. I've been skiing a lot with my family. I can get right up on my skis without any trouble. How about you?"

They kept talking as they headed for the door. And he stayed with her. Others were jammed in all around, and Darci caught sight of Bettina not far away. But Greg was definitely not looking in her direction.

"Hi, Greg," Bettina called out, but Greg just glanced around and waved.

Darci kept talking about waterskiing and her trips to the river with her family, and in a few minutes they were out in front of the Mess Hall. Bright, outside lights shone down on the boys and girls gathered in groups there, and Darci was glad all over again she'd worn makeup, as Ashley had suggested. The rain had stopped at last, and the night air felt cool and damp as they stood there, talking.

"How do you like this camp?" he wanted to know.

"I like it a lot," she told him. "And you know what else I like? Come on over here, and I'll show you."

Darci led him over to the office to show him the trophies in the window. "It'd be really fun to win one of these," she said.

"Yeah, they're the greatest," he said admiringly. "We have them, too, and our cabin got lucky and won them last year."

She wasn't a bit surprised. He seemed like the

type who would. "Will you win this year?" she asked, half-teasing.

"I will if you will," he teased her back.

Greg didn't seem in any hurry to leave, but finally some boys called to him. "Guess I better go, Darci. Hey, I'd sure like to see you again."

"Oh, yes," Darci said enthusiastically. "Me, too." Greg smiled, and Darci turned and plunged into the crowds, looking everywhere for Ashley. She had to find her, had to tell her about this meeting with Greg. Was Ashley still with Rolf? Could talking to Rolf possibly be as exciting as talking to Greg? Darci kept moving through the crowd, looking everywhere. But there were so many boys and girls scattered all over the place that she couldn't find Ashley.

Finally, Darci decided Ashley must have gone back to the cabin. She'd go there.

Darci raced off down the pathway toward the cabins. As she passed number 10, she noticed the door open and some of the girls already inside. So maybe Ashley *was* back at Cabin 13.

And as she raced up to her doorway, she saw the lights were on. "Ashley," she called out. "Listen to this." But when she opened the door, she found the cabin was empty. Well, she'd just have to wait till Ashley showed up. She went over to the mirror to admire her makeup again. She peered at herself. She leaned closer and stared, aghast.

"What is *that*?" she exclaimed out loud. A big blob of black mascara had dripped down her cheek. "Oh, no," she groaned. She grabbed a tissue and dabbed at it. Had she looked like this when she'd talked to Greg? She remembered how he'd smiled and smiled at her, how he'd said she looked so different tonight. Had he been laughing at her? Yes, she thought so.

She sank down on her bunk, feeling almost ready to cry. Suddenly she noticed a piece of paper on her pillow. Her name was printed on it. She wondered what it was. Who had left her a note? She picked it up, opened the folded piece of paper and read:

Darci, meet me in the woods behind the Mess Hall next Friday night. But keep it a secret. Greg.

"I can't believe it." Darci read the note three more times. "*Fan*-tastic!" She leapt to her feet. Greg wanted to see her again, and alone, too. She felt a thrill of excitement go through her. He must like her, he really must.

Just then the cabin door opened, and Ashley came in. "Ashley, I was looking all over for you.

Guess what?" Darci rushed toward her, holding out the note. "Look at this, will you? Isn't it terrific?"

Ashley took it and read it. "Fantastic! He likes you. See, I told you that makeup would do the job." Ashley fluttered her mascara-laden eyelashes and looked impressed.

"But isn't that kind of a funny place to meet?"

"No, it's a nice spot. There's a bench. Kids go and sit under the pines and stuff."

"And meet guys?"

Ashley rolled her eyes. "Why not? If they're lucky."

"Wow-e-e, Ashley." Darci burst into a laugh. "Isn't this really something?" Then she looked down at the note. "But how did he get it to me?"

Ashley shrugged. "Why worry? He probably asked one of the younger girls to put it in your cabin."

"Oh, right," Darci agreed. "When I was looking for you."

"Smart of him, wasn't it?" Ashley sounded admiring. "Wish he'd give Rolf the same idea."

"Won't he be breaking the rules to come over to the girls' camp?"

Ashley shrugged again. "That's his problem. Maybe he's got permission. Or maybe he's going to sneak over. Darci, just think. You've got a *date*."

Darci laughed. "I guess you could call it that."
Just then she heard the voices of the others outside the door and lowered her voice dramatically.
"Oh, Ashley, it's going to seem like forever until
next Friday."

6. I've Got It!

Darci was really busy all the next week with the usual tennis and swimming and volleyball. One day she went on a nature hike with Princess. Another day it was her turn to help clear the tables in the mess hall.

But always in the back of her mind was the thought that she had a date to meet Greg in the woods. What would it be like? She could hardly wait for the week to pass.

On Wednesday Babs announced at lunch that there was to be a softball game that afternoon. After lunch she led all the older girls up to the big open field behind the cabins, where she divided them into two teams.

"The odd-numbered cabins can be called the Greens," Babs called out, "and they'll play against the even-numbered ones." Darci glanced at her friends knowingly. They'd be playing against Bettina and her gang.

"Can we be called the Tens," Bettina spoke up quickly, "because we're in Cabin 10? Besides, it's an even number."

"Okay," Babs agreed, "and you can be the captain, Bettina."

Bettina smiled, as if she'd of course expected to be chosen. And Darci wondered who Babs would pick to be captain for the Greens. As a first-year girl, Darci knew she didn't have a chance, and for the same reason, neither did her cabinmates Sara and Julie.

But Babs chose Ashley for captain of the Greens, and then said, "In a few days we'll have a real game, instead of just practice games for fun."

"Great," Bettina called out. "That's what we want, a real game."

The Cabin 13 girls looked at one another. They knew what Bettina thought, that Cabin 10 was really good and would win. Darci wondered if the Greens had a chance.

When they were back in their cabin later, they all discussed it. Beating the Tens would be tough, they agreed. "You know how Bettina's always boasting about how good she is at softball," Darci said worriedly.

Ashley made a wry face. "I'm afraid Bettina really *is* good. She'll be the pitcher."

"I'm the pitcher on my team at home," Julie spoke up.

"Julie!" Darci and Ashley chorused in surprise.

"All *right*!" Ashley said. "I'm all-around okay, but pitching isn't really my thing, not like gymnastics."

"Me neither," Darci agreed. "But now we have a pitcher. Julie, that's so great you can do it. But listen, I have an idea. Why don't we get some practice?"

"Let's," Sara put in. "You don't play that much softball when you live in New York City."

After that, Darci and Ashley and Julie and Sara skipped the after-supper activities and went up to the softball field every evening. They'd do batting and catching, and Julie would pitch to them. On the way back they'd stop and admire the silver cups in the office window.

"Ooooh, they're so pretty." Julie longingly whistled air through the braces on her teeth.

"Maybe I'll draw a picture of them," Sara said with a giggle, "Just in case we don't win."

"Maybe we *will* win, who knows?" Darci said. "We're doing great, Gail says. Besides, it's other things, too, you know, sportsmanship and citizenship and all that."

"Sure. We're good at lots of things." Ashley grinned. "Meeting boys, too, right, Darci?"

They all laughed. Sara and Julie knew about Darci's coming date with Greg, but they hadn't told anyone else about it.

On Thursday, the day of the softball game, the whole camp came to the field to watch. It was a perfect spot for a game, a big open field with a row of blackberry bushes at the end, beneath a blue sky with fluffy, white clouds overhead. The younger girls spread out on the grass on the side- lines to watch, while the two teams took their positions on the field. Babs was the umpire.

"Who's going to win?" one of the younger girls called out.

"Keep watching and you'll see," Darci said. "Maybe the Greens will."

"No way. The Tens are going to win," Bettina shouted back, her eyes flashing.

The game began. Out on the pitcher's mound, Julie nervously licked her lips, but she looked strong and sure as she threw the ball. The only trouble was, when Bettina went out to pitch, she looked even stronger and more sure.

When Darci got up to bat she concentrated hard on the ball. Forget who is out there pitching, she told herself. Don't let Bettina rattle you. And she swung her bat, hit the ball, and ran to first base.

But after the first couple of innings, the Tens were ahead. Bettina's pitching was very good.

41

And Fran, on first base, had a quick way of catching the ball and tagging the runner out. Even so, Darci got another hit and made it to first again.

But Fran was not impressed. "You might as well forget it," she scoffed, standing a few feet off the base. "You guys don't have a chance."

"Sure we do," Darci shot back. But secretly, she wondered if they did.

Everyone was trying hard, that was clear, especially the Cabin 10 girls. Bettina kept talking to her friends, encouraging them. When Lana got up to bat, her sister, Fran, screamed at her, "Put some muscle into it, you wimp."

But Bettina called out. "That's okay, Lana. Take your time." Darci felt faintly surprised. Was Bettina being nice because she wanted to win? Or did she have a good side after all?

The Tens kept their early lead and they held onto it all through the game. In the fifth inning a Ten girl got up to bat and hit a long fly ball over Julie's head. Another Ten girl on third base ran home, bringing the score up to eight to six in favor of the Tens.

The next inning was the sixth and last. The Greens were desperate.

"C'mere, everybody," Ashley called. "We've got to talk."

The team huddled around her. "Look, kids, try

harder. This is it, the last inning," she begged them.

"Yes, let's get a couple of runs," Darci urged. "Even a tie wouldn't be bad."

"Yeah, right," the others agreed.

"Let's knock their socks off," Julie exclaimed.

And in the next inning they did do better. Two girls got good hits, though Fran caught the ball on first and put them out. Then Darci got up to bat and made a long drive out to center field. She raced past Fran on first and made it to second, then to third. The next batter, a girl named Michelle, hit the ball way out in the field, too, and Darci ran home. Another run for the Greens. And after a couple more batters made hits, Michelle ran home and scored, too.

"Yay-y-y," the Greens cheered noisily. "A tie!" Now the score was eight to eight.

Darci felt nervously hopeful. If they could hold that tie, it would be almost as good as a win!

But when the Tens went up to bat, they got three good base hits. The bases were loaded.

"No extra innings," Babs called out warningly.

So this would be it. And Darci, standing in the outfield, felt even tenser. They had to keep the Tens from scoring, and she chanted with her teammates, "Come on, Julie, strike 'em out!"

Like a champion, Julie did strike out the next

two batters. Now the bases were loaded with two outs. Just one more batter to go, Darci thought. But Bettina was up at bat. It seemed suddenly hot out on the field, and the air felt heavy with apprehension.

Bettina stepped cockily up to home plate, tossed back her dark hair, and took a practice swing with her bat.

"Wrap it up, Bettina," the Tens screamed. "Kill that ball! Hit a homer!"

Darci moved back, close to the row of blackberry bushes. If Bettina did hit it her way, it could be a long one. She dug her hand into her fielder's glove and waited tensely.

Julie, out on the pitcher's mound, was eyeing home plate. Then she leaned forward and hurled the ball. There came a sharp crack of the bat, earsplitting almost, it was so loud. Darci saw the ball fly high, fast as a bird, and it was coming her way. It would go out over her head, land in the blackberry bushes, be a beautiful home run. Oh, no, no!

Without thinking, Darci ran backwards, eyes fixed on the ball, her fielder's glove cupped upwards. If only she could catch the ball. She swerved. There it was over her head! She leaped high.

She had it, she had it! She came crashing down, into the scratchy blackberry bushes. They tore at her back, her arms, her legs. She felt on fire as she rolled over and over, trying to get out of the bushes.

At last she lay on her back, looking up at the blue sky. Did she still have the ball? She didn't dare move. She looked down at her arms and the glove still clasped across her stomach. There, deep in her glove, was the ball.

"I've got it," she screamed, struggling to her feet, and she held up her glove for all to see.

A terrific shout went up from her team, and the girls came running toward her. "Yay-y-y, Darci! Good for you, Darci! We tied 'em, tied 'em! Darci, you're terrific!"

Darci's team crowded around, cheering and hugging her. And it felt great, like being a winner. But then Bettina came up close to her and whispered in her ear.

"Are you sure you didn't drop that ball, Darci?"

"What?" Darci turned and stared into Bettina's cold, accusing green eyes. "Of course not! No way!" Darci exclaimed, shocked. "I had it the whole time."

Bettina just shrugged and hurried off after her friends. Darci stared after her. What a pain she was. Did she think Darci would actually *lie* about it?

7. Darci's Date

"Do you really think I ought to go?" Darci asked Ashley. It was after supper on Friday at last. Darci and Ashley were in their cabin, and Darci had just finished brushing her hair for the third time.

"Of course you should." Ashley nodded vigorously. "It'll be okay. You have to take chances, I always say."

"I wonder if Gail will let me." Darci frowned. "Maybe it would be better if you came with me. Two of us going on a nature walk would look more believable than one."

Ashley looked thoughtful. "You know, you could be right. Sure, I'll go. I could sort of fade off into the woods when Greg shows up."

"Good." Darci picked up her bird book. "At least I've been on two walks with Princess." Darci admired the way Princess walked softly through the woods in her moccasins, her long braid of hair hanging down her back.

"Do I look like a real bird-watcher?" Darci asked hopefully.

Ashley laughed. "Sure you do! Why don't I bring my binoculars, too? That'll make it look like a true nature walk." She sighed then. "Lucky you. Be sure you tell Greg you know somebody who'd like to meet Rolf the same way."

"Sure. Of course. I'll drop the hint." Darci felt a surge of excitement. It was really happening. She was going to meet Greg. If Gail let her, of course. And wasn't it okay to do this? How could she miss this chance?

"Oh, Ashley, I'm so excited!" They hurried out of their cabin and down the pathway toward the Mess Hall. Shrieks and screams floated on the air from the girls over by the volleyball net. The older girls were getting ready to play volleyball while the younger ones were gathering nearby to take turns pounding a tetherball.

"Gail has to say yes," Darci said nervously. She felt a sudden moment of panic. What if Gail said no?

"I bet she will. She'll even be impressed, you know?"

"I hope." Darci smiled at Ashley.

They walked across the clearing toward Gail,

who was lining up teams for the volleyball game. "Gail," Darci called out as they came up to her, "is it okay if we go for a nature walk instead of playing the games tonight? We won't go far, just up behind the Mess Hall." Maybe she really could look at some birds while she was there.

"A nature walk, huh?" Gail looked surprised but pleased, too. "Well, I guess so. You've been on some hikes with Princess, right?"

"Yes." Darci nodded. "But we won't go as far as she does."

"We'll stay in the woods right behind the Mess Hall," Ashley put in.

"Okay. Not for long, maybe an hour. It'll be getting dark after that." Gail glanced down at Darci's bird book. "Evening should be a good time to spot some birds."

"Yes, oh yes, I think it is," Darci said gratefully.

"Especially with my binoculars," Ashley added.

Some of the other girls had stopped talking and seemed to be just standing there listening, the Cabin 10 girls mainly. Darci had a sudden terrible worry. She hoped they wouldn't get the idea and decide to do the same thing.

"Okay, thanks, Gail. We'll be back soon." She turned to leave quickly.

"Be sure you don't go any further," Gail called after them.

"We won't," Darci promised, and she and Ashley hurried off.

It wasn't until they got safely behind the Mess Hall that they began to laugh and talk. "You were right," Darci said. "She did like the idea."

"Sure, I knew she would." Ashley was all confidence.

But it also made Darci feel guilty. She'd definitely have to look at some birds, too, while she was waiting to meet Greg, though she probably wouldn't have much time.

They walked quickly past the big, covered metal bins where the garbage was kept so the raccoons and other animals couldn't get at it. From the Mess Hall came the rattle of dishes and the voices of the kitchen staff and the girls on the clean-up crew. Darci was glad tonight wasn't her turn to clear the tables again. She didn't mind doing her share, of course, though she didn't particularly like it the day she'd had to help peel a whole mountain of potatoes — even though everyone had loved the mashed potatoes that night.

Darci and Ashley crossed the clearing behind the Mess Hall and headed for the clump of woods. Off in the distance the sun was setting behind the hills. They started up the path under the pines; it was darker and quieter there. Only the evening twitter of birds overhead and the crunching of pine needles underfoot could be heard.

Darci looked eagerly around, but there was no one in sight. "Why don't I take a look with your binoculars?" Darci asked Ashley.

"Sure." Ashley handed them to Darci. They both stood still while Darci put them up to her eyes.

"See anything? Anything good, I mean?" Ashley giggled.

"Lots of trees." Darci turned slowly, peering all around at the woods. There were birches and maples and pines. She tilted her head back. A black crow cawed noisily in a treetop and a bluebird flew in and out of the leaves of a maple tree. Then she looked back down at the woods all around her.

"No sign of Greg," she said. "But maybe it's too soon."

"Right. Besides, the bench place is probably where he'd want to meet you."

Now the path began to lead uphill, and their feet slipped on the pine needles. But pretty soon they came to a small, open place, and there was a long wooden bench.

"No sign of him." Darci tried to fight off a feeling of disappointment.

"Hm-m-m." Ashley stopped. "I know what. I

think I'll go on back down the hill and wait there for you. He might not like to see you brought someone else along. Here, you keep the binocs in case you want to look for him."

"Well, okay. I can't believe your being here would scare him off, but who knows?" She grinned at Ashley and went over to the bench. "I'll just sit here a while."

It was really quiet after Ashley left. Darci peered through the woods with the binoculars for a while. She saw a gray squirrel skitter up a tree. And there was a blue jay, calling harshly from a nearby pine. A moment later she spotted a brown-and-white bird with rosy coloring on its head. She thumbed through the bird book and discovered it was a purple finch, the state bird of New Hampshire. Darci whistled, trying to imitate the finch's bubbly, pretty song. Sitting here like this *was* practically as good as going on a nature walk.

But the sun's rays had disappeared now, and the sky was turning gray. Where was Greg? She looked around impatiently. Maybe this wasn't the right spot. She got up, decided to walk over toward the boys' camp. There was a big wire fence that ran between the two camps, but there was no path in that direction. She pushed her way through thick bushes. Partway there, she tripped on some vines and fell. When she finally reached the fence she saw no one at all in the woods behind the boys' camp.

She turned and made her way back to the bench, seeing a startled rabbit jump into the bushes up ahead. It could've been fun to sit here and look at birds and animals if she weren't worrying about Greg. She watched a flock of sparrows settle in the branches of a thin white birch tree.

Darci moved restlessly on the bench. She couldn't stay much longer. It was getting late.

From a distance she heard sharp whistles splitting the air. That meant the end of games. She would have to go. The hour was up, and she had to get back.

She rose reluctantly from the bench, looking all around in the shadowy woods. "Greg," she called softly. "Greg." But no one answered; only a bird sang nearby.

She could hardly believe all this. Her wonderful date wasn't even going to happen? Frowning, she set off on the path, following it down the hill.

"Darci." Ashley stepped out from some bushes, startling her. "Did he come?"

"No." Darci shook her head. "I waited on the bench for ages. I even went over to the fence and looked at the boys' woods." A sudden humiliating thought shot through her mind. "Oh, Ashley, do you think he was just playing a joke on me?"

"I don't know." Ashley put her arm around Darci's shoulders. "Maybe he just couldn't get away."

"Do you think so?" Darci tried to believe that. "It's such a let-down," she confessed. "It makes me mad, too."

"Don't let it bother you, Darci." Ashley was comforting. "I bet he had a good reason."

"Well, he better." Darci frowned. "I hope he didn't just forget. Anyway, thanks for coming, Ashley."

They hurried down the path and back out of the woods. It had been a disappointing date, all right, and sort of embarrassing to be hanging around in the woods to meet someone who never showed up. She was really glad she hadn't told anyone outside her own cabin.

It was strange. Greg had seemed like such a friendly guy, someone you could believe. Now she didn't know what to think. She felt sad and cross all at the same time.

She'd have to try to find out what had happened to him.

8. Square Dance

On the camp bulletin board there was posted a big sign.

SQUARE DANCE TONIGHT
BOYS FROM BIRCH CAMP
WILL BE OUR GUESTS.

Darci and Ashley and some others crowded around to read it.

"Fantastic!" Ashley crowed. "What a chance to see Rolf." She poked Darci. "And you can see. . . ." She stopped. Others might hear. Besides, they both knew who she meant.

"Terrific! Great!" the older girls behind them were saying.

"Ugh, boys! Do we have to dance with boys?" some younger ones protested.

"We always have a square dance," another voice

said. And Darci turned around to see Bettina and her friend Fran beside her.

"You'll probably see your friend Greg," Fran said loudly to Bettina with a big smile.

"Do you know him very well?" Darci couldn't keep from saying.

"Of course." Bettina's green eyes looked cool. "He was here last year. He's older, you know." She smiled in a superior way and walked off with Fran as if she couldn't be bothered talking to Darci any longer.

All day Darci kept thinking about it — the dance, the way Bettina acted, why Greg hadn't met her. As she smashed the tennis ball across the court, she told herself, forget that Greg, anyway. Who wanted to know a boy who didn't show up for a date? But the hurt would come back all over again. Maybe she didn't belong at camp. Maybe it really was easier for people who'd been coming for years and years.

Yet when she and Ashley were swimming in the lake and gliding along in the cool water, talking and laughing, Darci realized how much she liked camp. And maybe Greg had had a good reason. Then a streak of excitement ran through her. Tonight she'd have a chance to be with him, and she could find out. But what if he was busy with Bettina the whole time?

"Do you want to borrow my makeup again?" Ashley asked Darci that evening as they were getty ready for the Square Dance. They were allowed to wear their own clothes tonight instead of the green-and-white camp clothes. And Darci had just pulled on her pink blouse and skirt.

"Say," Ashley added admiringly, "that pink looks good with your brown eyes and hair. How about some mascara and blusher and stuff to go with it?"

"Thanks, Ashley," Darci said. "But I think I won't try it tonight." Just maybe, she thought, she'd be dancing a lot and she didn't want a blob of mascara to come sliding down her face again.

"You look terrific," Darci added, looking over at her friend. Ashley was wearing her big, red earrings again with a matching red-and-white blouse and skirt.

"Thanks. Hope Rolf thinks so." She grinned at Darci. "I'm almost ready as soon as I put these on." She sank down on the edge of her bunk and began to pull on a pair of pantyhose.

"Oh, lucky you," Darci exclaimed, admiring the way they looked on Ashley's legs. "I didn't bring any hose to camp with me."

"They'll just make you hotter," Julie said, brushing her shiny, straight black hair. She tucked a checked shirt into her jeans. Julie didn't like to dress up.

"And you could get holes in them anyway," Sara pointed out. Sara was wearing jeans, too, and a T-shirt with a purple-flowered design on it, which she'd made in crafts.

"I know you're right," Darci said sadly. "Still, I wish I had some." They'd have made her look older, for one thing, just in case she did get a chance to talk to Greg. And if she did get that chance, she'd tell him she wasn't some little kid who could be ignored and stood up like that.

Gail, who was dressed and standing by the door, waiting for the girls, walked over to her footlocker. "Listen, Darci, if you really want some pantyhose, I have an old pair here. If you'd like to borrow them that'd be fine with me. But let's hurry. We want to be on time, gang."

"Oh, Gail, thanks a lot." Darci was delighted. "I'd love to, and I'll hurry." Darci quickly took the pantyhose from Gail and pulled them on. They were a little loose so she rolled them over inside the waistband of her skirt.

At last they were all ready. They hurried out the door together. Overhead the sky was dark, and a few stars glittered through the tall pines.

As they walked along Darci saw that the other girls looked dressed up, too, some in skirts, some in fancy blouses with jeans. Darci caught a glimpse of Fran and Lana up ahead in matching blouses and plaid skirts and Bettina in an all-white outfit.

Darci shivered. Would it be fun? Would Greg explain, and then they'd be friends again?

They were crossing the clearing, going past the camp office. In the window the trophies gleamed in the darkness. Would being a good square dancer help win a trophy? Well, why not?

When they reached the Mess Hall, Gail opened the door and turned to look them over. "You're looking good, girls. Have a lot of fun. I'll see you later."

Inside the Mess Hall Darci glanced around the crowded room, filled with boys and girls. All the tables and chairs had been pushed back against the wall, and cookies and punch were on one of the tables. Where was the tall, blond boy with blue eyes?

"Darci," Ashley said in her ear. "Look over there, across the room."

"Oh, yes, thanks. I see him. I'm going right over there and find out — " Darci broke off. Through the crowd she saw a girl with dark hair dressed in all-white outfit rush up to Greg and start laughing and talking rapidly. "Oh, no," Darci groaned. "Bettina beat me to it."

Babs blew her whistle then and yelled out to the crowd, "Find your partners, everybody."

Some of the kids groaned. "Let's eat first." But Babs just shook her head and started up loud square-dance music on a tape deck.

"Hi, Rolf," Darci heard Ashley call out and watched as Ashley joined hands with tall, freckle-faced Rolf.

Then a short, chubby guy appeared before Darci. "Hi. My name is Michael. You wanna dance?" he asked.

Darci supposed she did. "Sure, thanks. I'm Darci." And if she got to pass Greg in the circle she'd just give him a cold look and she'd whisper, "Where were you, anyway?"

Loud square-dance music filled the room, and Babs yelled out, "All right, kids, join hands and circle wide." Darci tried not to look over at Bettina in her all-white outfit next to Greg. Besides, the music was speeding up and so was the circle. They were whirling around, skirts flying, feet skipping, kids laughing. Darci loved to feel herself moving this way and that to the music. And Michael was a good dancer.

But where was Greg? Wasn't she going to get a chance to pass him?

"Promenade your partner," Babs shouted, "two by two. Swing your partner 'round and 'round." But still, Greg seemed to be always on the other side of the circle.

The music was stopping. Then Babs called out, "Change your partners, everybody."

Change partners? The words rang in Darci's head. Of course, now was her chance. "Thanks, Michael. It was fun." She threw him a fast smile, then moved off. Maybe she'd ask Greg to dance, then find out just why he hadn't come to the woods. He was standing over there. Was he looking around, too? Maybe he was trying to find her and wanted to explain it all. She raced toward him. Suddenly he moved and she almost crashed into him. Again.

"Uh, hi," she said.

"Hi, yourself," he said. To her surprise he gave her a big, friendly smile, and then he said, "So how're you doing? Rolf told me you made quite a catch in the softball game."

She felt pleased he'd heard about it. "Oh, yes. I landed in the blackberry bushes, see?" Darci held out her scratched-up arms as proof. "I was really lucky."

"Say, that must've been a good catch, all right." He looked so friendly and interested, she couldn't think how to begin talking about the note.

Besides, just then Babs yelled out to everyone, "Ready? Honor your partner by your side. All join hands and circle wide."

"Come on, Darci. Let's dance." Greg grabbed her hand.

"Uh, okay." She couldn't get over feeling surprised. He certainly seemed glad to see her. Before she could speak, a blast of music filled the room, and they all began to slide around in a circle. There was no more chance for talking now.

"Honor your partner and give her a swing," Babs called out. This was terrific, Darci thought, as she slipped her arm through Greg's, her pink skirt whirling around, her stocking-clad legs moving fast beneath her.

"All right," Babs called, "take the left arm and swing her 'round."

Darci hooked her left arm through Greg's, that super-tanned arm, and began to whirl the other way. This was like a dream almost. Darci caught a glimpse of Ashley's black hair flying by as she danced with Rolf, and Sara's glasses shining in the light, and Julie's metallic grin at Michael.

"Face the gal on the other side," Babs shouted. "Swing her fast and move on around, all around the circle you go." Darci hooked arms with all these other boys as she went round the circle. She hadn't asked Greg any questions yet. Well, she would just as soon as the music stopped.

When Babs called out something about do-se-do, then home you go and everybody swing, Darci found herself coming back around the circle to Greg. "Okay," she told herself. "Get ready."

The music stopped, and Darci stood beside Greg, panting a little. Another girl and boy came up to them and stood talking a minute. Finally, after they left Darci turned to Greg.

"Greg," she said, looking up at him. "I have to ask you something. It's about a note I found on my bunk." She thought she could see surprise in his blue eyes.

"What are you talking about, Darci? What note?"

Now Babs began shouting out commands again. "All right, everybody. Form two long lines. This way, over here. Stand opposite your partner."

Everyone began to shuffle around, and Darci and Greg had to move with the crowd. Darci followed along in a daze. She could hardly think about what she was doing, she was so dumbfounded. Greg had said, "What note?" He didn't know about it! Then who did?

"Take that little gal and swing her along," Babs called.

Now Greg was taking her hands and they were

dancing down between the two long lines of smiling, watching faces. She and Greg were doing sort of a skip-jog, skip-jog and whirl-and-turn, whirl-and-turn.

But all of a sudden something terrible was happening. Darci's legs felt odd. Something was bagging and slipping and sliding. Darci glanced down. Oh, no! She clutched her hips. Then the tops of her legs. She grabbed for the sliding pantyhose. But oh, too late, too late! The pantyhose were all twisting and bunching and falling down, down. And there were laughing faces everywhere. Even over the music she could hear that huge burst of laughter. She looked ridiculous, just ridiculous! She had to get out of here.

Yanking up her stockings, she pushed her way through the laughing crowd, past all the grinning faces, and rushed out the door of the Mess Hall and down the pathway to her cabin.

That night she lay in her bunk for a long time, listening to the others breathing. Her mind kept going over the whole disastrous evening — how everyone had laughed. Darci could feel her face turn bright red right there in the darkness. Greg must think she was a real loser to let her pantyhose fall down like that.

And then she remembered something else about

the evening. Greg hadn't known about that note. Who had written it? She tossed and turned under her covers, worrying.

How she wished she were back in her own room and bed and could hear her parents' voices talking downstairs! But she was far away from home now, here in Cabin 13. Could there be anything to that silly superstition that thirteen meant bad luck?

Gradually Darci became calmer. She heard the low hoot of an owl out in the woods. She noticed how peaceful and quiet it was in the cabin and how the silver moonlight was falling softly through the windows and making bright squares on the floor. And finally, Darci slept.

9. A Bad Case

But in the morning when she awoke she felt restless, and she found herself scratching her arms, then her legs. And why did her face feel so funny, as if a thousand ants were crawling on it? What was going on?

Darci threw back her covers and jumped out of bed. She rushed over to the mirror and peered into it. Why, her face was all red and swollen and rashy. She pulled up the sleeves of her pajamas, and she had an itchy rash all over her arms, too, and oh, help, it was on her legs. She groaned out loud.

"What's the matter, Darci?" Gail sat up in her bunk.

"Hey, what's going on?" Ashley tossed back her covers, too, her black hair a tousled mass around her head.

"Look at me." Darci turned to face them.

Gail came hurrying over to her. "Oh, no! Darci,

you poor kid. It looks like you've got poison ivy!"

Now Julie and Sara were sitting up in their bunks, too. "What's up? Is somebody sick?" Julie asked.

Darci moaned again. "This is worse. I've got poison ivy, I guess." Suddenly she remembered when she went to the woods and left the path to look through the fence. She'd fallen in some vines.

"Oh, Darci," Ashley exclaimed, making a face. Darci knew Ashley must be wondering about their trip to the woods, too.

"Well, that's really too bad," Gail said. "You'll have to go see Mrs. Burkett. She can give you some stuff to put on it."

"Mrs. Burkett?" Darci echoed, suddenly worried. What if Mrs. Burkett asked her a lot of questions?

"You need to get it under control. Tomorrow night there's a big camp fire, and the guys from Birch Camp are coming, too, remember? And I was hoping some of you could put on an entertainment, you know, sing, tell a story, something like that."

Darci and her cabinmates looked at one another in surprise. "What could we do?" Darci wondered out loud, almost forgetting her poison ivy for a minute.

"I thought, since I've got such a great cabin this year . . . and of course, the other campers will be doing things." Gail broke off and looked at them hopefully.

Darci glanced in the mirror at herself. She looked far too awful to stand up in front of everybody!

"I could do gymnastics if I had a gym." Ashley grinned and began to get dressed.

"I drew pictures in front of my class one time," Sara added, "but it'd be hard for anyone to see them at night."

Darci started to pull on her green-and-white camp clothes. The thought of standing up in front of both camps with poison ivy all over her face made her cringe. Still, Gail wanted them to do something, she could tell.

Just then Darci's glance happened to fall on her bird book on the floor there by her bunk. She'd gone on another long nature walk yesterday and seen lots of birds.

"I suppose I could talk about birds," she said hesitantly. How pleased her parents would be if they knew the bird book was turning out to be so useful.

"Hmmm." Gail looked thoughtful. "That's an idea. Would you, Darci?"

"But I look so awful." Darci took another look in the mirror at her red, rashy face and almost wished she had kept quiet.

"Well, as Sara says, it will be dark. I hear two of the girls in Cabin 10 are going to sing," Gail added slyly.

"Oh, Darci, do it, do it," Ashley urged.

"Yeah, please, Darci," Julie said. "We'll all clap for you, too."

"Well, I don't even know if I'd be any good," Darci protested, but the bell rang for breakfast, and nobody was listening now. The others were all bustling around, dressing, making up their bunks, stowing shoes in a straight line and generally tidying up. As Darci hurried to finish up, too, she thought of something else. It would give her a chance to see Greg again. She could ask him once more about that note. Maybe she could stay in the shadows so he couldn't get a good look at her.

As everyone left the cabin and went up the path together, Darci began to worry about seeing Mrs. Burkett. What would Mrs. Burkett say to her? One of the rules here was not to go off the trails anywhere when out in the woods. And Darci had.

"It's okay," Ashley whispered in her ear as they neared the camp office, although Darci knew it wasn't, not really. But she gave Ashley a grateful look anyway. Ashley was a loyal friend.

As she turned in the office she thought of the trophies. What if she got into trouble now and ruined her cabin's chances?

Luckily, Mrs. Burkett seemed to be in a hurry that morning. She was just coming out the office door when Darci arrived.

"My, oh my," she said, examining Darci's rash in the doorway. "You have got a bad case of poison ivy. I don't think you've been careful about where you've walked." She looked at Darci reproachfully, and Darci couldn't think of what to say.

"Come, I'll give you some medicine." Mrs. Burkett turned back into the office and went over to a cabinet. "Here you go." She handed Darci a bottle and a tube of ointment. "Take these antihistamines, one at night, one in the morning. And remember, you can give your poison ivy to other people just by touching them. It's very contagious, so be careful! Here's some lotion to rub on the rash."

"Thank you, Mrs. Burkett." Darci wondered if there was any chance these things could make it all go away by tomorrow night.

"Remember where you walk next time, Darci," Mrs. Burkett added reproachfully. "And take care of that rash, all right?"

"Yes, yes, I will," Darci promised fervently.

"Be sure you do, Darci. Now I've got to go speak to a meeting of the staff." And Mrs. Burkett hurried off.

Relieved that Mrs. Burkett hadn't asked any questions about how Darci had gotten poison ivy, she followed Mrs. Burkett out the door. As she crossed the clearing she paused by the bulletin board to read the notice about the camp fire. How could she have fun at the camp fire with this rash all over?

Just then she heard voices behind her and she glanced back. There were Bettina and her cab-inmates, coming toward her.

"Oh, Darci, that was so-o-o funny when your pantyhose fell down last night!" Bettina called out, a huge grin on her face. "Greg really laughed his head off." She stopped in front of Darci. Gillian and Fran and Lana crowded around, too, all of them wearing their leather friendship bracelets as usual, Darci noticed.

But before Darci could speak, Bettina leaned toward her. "Euw-w-w, what's happened to you? How *gross*." Bettina rolled her eyes.

"It's only poison ivy," Darci said stiffly.

"You've really got a bad case of it." Gillian smoothed her lopsided hairdo, then glanced quickly toward Bettina.

70

"I wonder how you got it," Fran said with a little knowing smile on her face.

Were they all in on it? What if *Bettina*, not Greg had written the note? Looking at them, Darci decided she was not going to admit that she'd caught the poison ivy as a result of a note, whoever sent it. And if they didn't know about the note, she certainly wasn't going to tell them.

So she said, "Probably I caught it when I made that catch in softball the other day. Remember, when we tied you guys?"

A look of annoyance crossed Bettina's face. Then she shrugged. "But that was days ago. Didn't you go on a nature walk just the other night?" She watched Darci closely, a satisfied expression on her face.

Yes, Darci thought. She could be the one who wrote that note, all right.

"I'm really interested in bird-watching, you know." No way were these girls going to find out from her why she really went up into the woods, Darci decided. "Gail wants me to give a speech about it at the camp fire," she added. She couldn't resist boasting a little to them.

Bettina said, "Cabin 10 has really good singers, and Lana plays the guitar."

Was singing better than talking? Darci felt a

stab of worry, but she tried not to show it. "Well, I've got to get going." She turned to walk coolly away, though inside she was really burning. She was almost convinced Bettina and the Cabin 10 gang had written that note.

Then an even more terrible idea struck her. Maybe they were all in on it — Greg, too!

10. Camp Fire

Darci told her cabinmates about her talk with the Cabin 10 girls during free-swim period, as they were all bobbing around in a circle together out on the lake. They were outraged to think Bettina and her friends might have been behind the note.

"Of course, they wouldn't admit it!" Ashley pushed her wet black hair off her forehead and looked cross. "They're disgusting. But I'll bet they did it. I think we should get back at them."

"How?" Sara asked.

"We could catch a frog here in the lake and put it in Bettina's bed." Ashley grinned.

Julie squirted water through her teeth, then frowned. "Wait a minute. I don't think that'd be very fair to the frog."

"You could ask Greg again, just to be sure." Sara rolled onto her back and began to float, her face tipped thoughtfully up to the sky.

"Yes, I was going to at the camp fire tonight. If you think of any other ideas, let me know." Darci looked around at her circle of friends. If it weren't for the Cabin 10 girls, camp would be nearly perfect, she thought — except for the poison ivy! She dove way deep down in the lake, letting the cool water rush over her. It felt good on her itchy rash.

But when it came time to get ready that evening, Darci groaned as she looked in the mirror. The pills Mrs. Burkett had given her did help the itching of the poison ivy, true. But the rash still looked awful. What could she do?

Darci put on her dark glasses, then pulled a visor cap down low over her face. Next she tied a scarf around her neck so she could sink her rashy chin in it. Only her cheeks showed and they were okay. Well, she'd give her speech fast, then fade away into the shadows. Somehow, she'd have to get hold of Greg and manage to stay back under the trees and out of the light.

Sara came over and looked at her and giggled. "Oh, Darci, you look like someone in disguise, a spy maybe."

Darci frowned at herself in the mirror. "I know I look pretty strange, but I have to try *something*. Maybe everyone will think this is the way bird-watchers dress."

"Of course," Sara said loyally. "Don't worry."

Going outside, the Cabin 13 girls joined the others as they streamed along the pathway toward the clearing. Down by the lake huge flames from the bonfire danced high in the darkness and cast a bright light everywhere. And all the boys and girls crowded around, their faces clearly revealed in the firelight.

Seeing the bright fire, Darci hung back. "Ashley, I think I'll stay here in the shadows for now." Ashley nodded understandingly. Then Darci spotted Greg, his blond hair shining in the firelight, and she saw sneaky non-rashy Bettina hurrying forward to talk and laugh with him. What were they laughing about? The note trick? Darci squirmed, thinking about it.

"Oh, Ashley, how am I going to face everybody?"

"Darci, you have to, for our cabin," Ashley answered. "We can't let that Cabin 10 gang get ahead of us." Darci knew she was right.

Some girls from Cabin 7 got up and did a little dance, and everybody cheered afterwards. Then Rolf and another boy stood up and told jokes. Some younger girls were up next and sang the Pine Tree Camp song. Then the Cabin 10 girls gathered in a circle around Lana, who began to strum her guitar. As they sang, Darci quickly realized they were good. Their voices were clear, and they stayed in harmony surprisingly well. Lana played with real rhythm and every once in a while smiled shyly at the audience.

Everyone cheered and clapped the loudest yet.

When it was over, Ashley leaned toward Darci. "I have to admit they weren't bad."

Darci nodded. "I'm afraid you're right," she whispered back. Darci felt worse and worse. Her hands were cold and her face was hot. Was there any way her talking could be as good as their singing?

Now Gail was coming through the crowd toward her and calling out, "Darci, come on. Your turn."

Nervously, Darci made her way through the crowd up to the edge of the fire.

"How come the dark glasses?" a boy called out. "Have you got pinkeye?" There was loud laughter. Darci tried to ignore it and all the faces, everywhere, all turned in her direction, all looking at her. One of them must be Greg.

She edged back from the bright fire so her rash wouldn't be so easy to see. "I'm a bird-watcher," she began. "Out in the woods around us are some terrific birds, bluebirds and blue jays, robin redbreasts and little gray-brown wrens. And then there's a brown-and-white bird with a rosy-colored head. It's the purple finch, the state bird of

New Hampshire." She went on to describe some of the birds further, what they liked to eat and where they liked to build their nests. Everyone was quiet at least while she talked, which she hoped was a good sign. She ended by whistling an imitation of the finch's song, its quick melodic notes.

Campers applauded as she finished, and a few kids did some whistling of their own. Darci slipped back into the crowd, eager to disappear. "That was really good, Darci," a few girls and boys said. Darci felt relieved. She began to look anxiously about, wondering how she could get hold of Greg.

She eased back to the edge of the crowd, where the shadows were deeper. Now where was Greg? She was just peering all around when she heard a voice say, "Looking for someone?"

She whirled around. It was Greg! And even in the darkness she could see how cute he was, tall and blond-haired.

"Oh, hi. I wanted to see you," she blurted out.

"You did?" he said. His white teeth flashed in a smile in the darkness. "I was hoping I could find you. I liked your talk just now."

"Oh, thanks. I really like birds. I go out in the woods to bird-watch a lot." She wanted to emphasize that, just in case Bettina had told him about tricking her with that note. At least he wouldn't think she went to the woods just to meet him.

"Sa-a-ay," he exclaimed, bending toward her. "What're you doing with the sunglasses? Is the bonfire too bright for you?" She could hear the amusement in his voice.

She stepped back nervously. "I was trying to look like a bird-watcher. But the fire is hot — and I like it better back in the shadows, don't you?" She stepped further back.

"You do?" Why did he sound so surprised? "Well, look, it's even darker over here. Come on this way, Darci."

She followed him over under some trees, where it was really dark. Glancing up at the tree branches overhead, she could see the stars through the leaves, bright and shiny in a dark sky. "Look at all the stars," she said.

"Oh . . . yeah," he said. A small silence fell between them.

"Greg, remember I told you about a note I found on my bunk? Are you sure you don't know anything about it?" She couldn't believe he did. She hoped he didn't.

"No, Darci, no way. That sounds like the usual camp jokester. There's always one of them around. What was it about anyway?"

"Oh, nothing much," Darci managed to say.

Somehow, she felt certain he was telling the truth, that he wouldn't play such a trick on her.

From up by the bonfire they could hear someone playing some really great songs on a guitar. "Say, listen to the guitarist," Greg exclaimed. "It's a kid named Jake. Doesn't he sound terrific?"

Darci was afraid Greg would suggest they go up there where they could see and hear better. "Yes, he does, especially from a distance. It's sort of fun, to hear music float on the air, don't you think?"

"Yeah, definitely better from back here," he agreed quickly.

She glanced up at the stars again and this time she noticed a bright moon coming up through the treetops. "And look at the moon," she said.

Greg looked up. "Oh, yeah, yeah. It's great, all right." All of a sudden he was moving toward her. "Darci," he murmured, and his arm went around her. Then he had both arms around her, and he was bending toward her, and he was coming closer and closer.

Oh, help, he was going to kiss her! She should have known better than to talk about stars and moons. Now she'd have to tell him about her poison ivy.

"Wait, Greg! I have to tell you something." He straightened a little.

"Hm-m-m?" he murmured.

"Oh, Greg, I've got poison ivy. It's all over my face and arms, and you might catch it."

To her surprise, Greg burst out laughing. "Is that what the disguise is for, Darci? It's not just for bird-watching, after all? But listen." Now he came close again. "I'm not afraid of catching it."

"You're not?" she breathed, tipping her face up toward him. If he didn't care, then why should she?

"Uh-uh," he murmured. His face came closer and closer, and she shut her eyes, waiting. She'd only had one real kiss ever before in her life, and now maybe she was about to have another one.

But all of a sudden there was a burst of wild giggling behind them. Darci's eyes flew open, and she jumped back from Greg. Bettina and Fran were there, lurking over near some bushes. Why did they have to show up just now?

Greg shrugged. "Guess we drew an audience, eh, Darci?"

Darci just shook her head. Wouldn't you know, it was the Cabin 10 girls making things tough for her, as usual. They could be envious, of course. Either one of them would probably love to be in her spot back here with Greg now. But she didn't want to stay if they were here, too.

She turned to Greg. "Come on, Greg. Why don't

we go listen to the music?" They'd find some shadows to stand in, away from the light of the camp fire. It wouldn't be like this though, just the two of them, under the trees and looking at the moon. She didn't know when it would ever be like this again.

11. Who Did It?

While they were cleaning up their cabin the next morning, Darci told her cabinmates about being with Greg at the camp fire. "And you know what? While we were standing back in the shadows he kept coming closer and closer to me." They all stopped working to listen.

"Do you think he was going to kiss you?" Sara flopped down on her unmade bunk and looked impressed.

"And you think Bettina saw?" Ashley began to smile. "That serves her right. Because I still think she's the one who wrote that note. After all, Greg has said twice now that he didn't do it."

"That's true." Darci nodded. He had sounded pretty definite, all right. "And who else could've done it?" She remembered some younger girls who'd teased her about Greg a few times. Was it possible they wrote it?

"I suppose we could flat-out ask Bettina, but

she'd deny it, I bet." Ashley started to gather up a bunch of wet towels from the floor.

Suddenly Darci had an idea. She dropped the bundle of socks and shorts she'd been holding and rushed over to her footlocker.

Rummaging around in it, she found the note she'd hidden there. She held it up and read it again.

"Look," she said to the others. "See these backward e's, the way they're printed?"

"Yeah." Sara bent over the note, peering closely through her glasses. "They look almost like threes. Some people print that way." The others crowded around to take a look, too.

"Well," Ashley said, "*that's* interesting."

"You can say that again," Julie exclaimed. "Who *does* print like that?"

They all stared at one another for a minute. It was very quiet.

"We could take a chance and go look around Cabin 10 when no one's there," Ashley suggested. "We might see somebody's mail lying around or something."

"Hm-m-m." Darci frowned. The idea didn't appeal to her exactly. Then she snapped her fingers. "I know what. We could try watching when Mrs. Burkett collects the mail today." Mrs. Burkett always took the campers' mail into town, the little village of Camden, not far away, to mail it. "Would you all help me?"

"Count me in," Ashley nodded her head vigorously.

"Me, too," Julie agreed.

"We'll each stick near one of the Cabin 10 girls," Sara added, her eyes excited.

"Great!" Darci smiled at her friends.

"We'll get them yet, Darci," said Ashley. "Watch out, Cabin 10!"

That day at lunch Darci and her friends hurried over to the Mess Hall early. When it was time to line up for mail call at Mrs. Burkett's table, they managed to be right behind the Cabin 10 girls, who were so busy talking loudly about how they might get mail from boys at home they didn't pay any attention to Darci and her cabinmates. And filing past the big, open box for outgoing mail, they had a perfect view of the letters.

But, alas, Bettina had nothing to mail that day. And the handwriting on her friends' letters didn't look like the writing on the note.

"Rotten luck," Ashley muttered in Darci's ear. "Too bad Bettina didn't have a letter we could look at."

"I know." Darci frowned. "Maybe we can check her mail another day."

She was still disappointed about it as they all streamed out of the Mess Hall after lunch, even though it was such a nice, sunny day with blue skies and tall, green pines overhead. But Darci felt more cheerful when two younger girls came running up to her and said, "Hi, Darci, that was a great talk last night about birds."

"Thanks, thanks a lot," Darci answered. At least all the other girls here at Pine Tree Camp were friendly. And now she felt sure Greg hadn't tried to trick her. In fact, thinking about Greg made her feel pretty good.

"Oh, look," Ashley said as they crossed the clearing. "What's up?" A bunch of girls were huddled in front of the bulletin board.

"Looks like news," Darci said as they hurried to join the crowd.

Over the heads of the others they could see a big sheet of paper tacked up, with a list of names on it.

"What's going on?" Darci asked.

"It's a canoe race," a freckled-faced girl said. "You're supposed to sign up if you want your cabin to be in it."

Darci and Ashley looked at each other. "What do you think?" Darci asked Ashley. She wished she'd done more canoeing.

"Oh, let's." Ashley looked excited. "My mom and I have a canoe at home and we go out on the lake near our house a lot."

"Perfect, Ashley!" Darci beamed at her friend. They moved up to the bulletin board to sign their names.

As Darci was writing hers, she glanced at some of the names above. Suddenly, an idea hit her. "Ashley," she whispered. "Here are a lot of signatures."

Ashley's eyes widened. "Oh, yeah." And though others were waiting and saying, "Hurry, we have to get to volleyball," Darci and Ashley scanned the names, or at least, all the e's in the names.

They both saw it at the same time. There, near the top, was Bettina Bentley. But the e's looked just like normal e's, no different from all the others. And underneath her name was Fran Penelli's name and it was okay, too.

Darci stepped back from the crowd, feeling let down. "Too bad," she said. "It would've been nice to find out."

"Right," Ashley agreed, frowning thoughtfully. "I still think it was Bettina. Maybe she faked her handwriting when she wrote you that note."

"Say, that is an idea, isn't it?" Darci said. They started across the clearing. "Anyway, I don't know just what I'd do if I did find out."

"Get back at her, I'd say," Ashley said. orously.

"True," Darci agreed. "She's caused me a lot of trouble." She ran her hands across her face where the poison ivy rash was at last fading.

As they walked by the camp office, they stopped to look at the silver trophies in the window.

"You know," Ashley said, "the Cabin 10 gang are just sure they're going to win these. That's what bugs me. Those girls act so superior all the time."

The silver gleamed in the morning sunlight. Darci looked at the trophies a minute more and thought again how nice one would look on the shelf at home along with her family's trophies. True, her brother's trophies were all figures of baseball and soccer players. But Mom's and Dad's tennis ones were silver cups just like these. Hers would fit right in.

Darci turned to Ashley. "You know how we could really get back at Cabin 10?" She paused, a feeling of determination sweeping over her. "By winning these things."

12. Yay, We Won!

Darci and Ashley were excited about being in the canoe race. Darci wished she'd had more experience, but at least she'd learned how to paddle a canoe this summer. Julie and Sara hadn't learned as well yet, so that meant Darci and Ashley would be paddling the canoe for Cabin 13. Each cabin would be represented by one canoe in the race.

"You and I are both pretty light, so that should help," Ashley told Darci. "Bettina and Fran are bigger," she added with a grin. Bettina and Fran had entered the race for Cabin 10.

"So maybe we do have some hope of winning!" Darci exclaimed. It would be so great if they could. That would show those Cabin 10 girls a thing or two.

Just that morning Gail had said, "This cabin is really all right. You guys are doing okay, no kid-

88

ding. You might have a real chance at winning the trophies."

Every day Darci and Ashley, along with all the others, went down to the lake, donned bulky life jackets and went out in the canoes. Babs cruised around in the motorboat, keeping an eye on all of them. Even though the midsummer days were hot, Darci felt cool and relaxed on the water.

And out there, just the two of them in their canoe, Darci could forget all about that trick note and the embarrassing stockings. Instead, she remembered her last meeting with Greg, and that made her feel better, too.

Darci had to smile a little, thinking how she and Greg had been together in the evening shadows. But would she get to see him again? When? Camp would be ending pretty soon.

The day of the race was sunny, with a slight breeze now and then. Everyone who was signed up for it gathered down by the dock, talking and laughing. Bettina kept telling the others how she and Fran had won the canoe race the year before.

"And I came in second, don't forget," Michelle put in.

"This may not be so easy," Darci whispered to Ashley.

"I know." Ashley shrugged. "But I think I learned some things about racing last year, and

I've been doing all that canoeing with my mom at home. I think I'd better sit in the stern, Darci, and you be up front. That way I can do most of the steering."

"Okay," Darci agreed. She was relieved Ashley knew so much about it.

A moment later Babs blew a whistle and called out, "All right, kids, the race is to the south end of the lake. That way." She motioned with her arm. "There are two buoys. Go between them. That will be the finish line. I'll be watching from the motorboat. Now come get your canoes. And remember, stay out of each other's way."

They all milled out onto the dock, pulled on the life jackets, and climbed into the green fiberglass canoes. Darci scrambled forward to take her seat up front in the bow. Ashley settled in the stern. They pushed off from the dock and paddled over to the starting line. A slight breeze rippled across the water and blew in their faces, and the canoe rocked gently on the lake.

Babs came motoring out in her boat and stopped near the group of canoes.

"Be ready, Darci," Ashley called to her in a low voice. "When she blows that whistle, dig in."

"Okay, I will," Darci promised over her shoulder. She gripped her paddle, braced her feet on the bottom of the canoe, then watched Babs intently. In a moment Babs stood up and raised the whistle to her lips, the wind ruffling her short, dark hair.

"Get set," Babs yelled in her husky voice. Then she blew the whistle, and the sound blasted through the air. Darci plunged her paddle in the water, pulled it back hard, lifted it dripping out of the water and leaned forward for the next stroke. The boat shot ahead. They were already skimming along. She chanted to herself, dip, paddle, pull, dip, paddle, pull.

"Darci, great, keep it up," Ashley panted from behind her, and Darci did. Already some canoes were behind them. Then, oh, no, Darci faltered and made a splash with her paddle. "Be careful," Ashley warned.

But now they were going fast again. The wind blew water up into Darci's face, and it felt good. On the shore ahead the leaves on the trees were shimmering and fluttering, and the trees were bending. Halfway there!

Now Darci dared to glance around quickly. She and Ashley were ahead of all the other canoes, but one. And that one was almost alongside, and Darci caught a glimpse of Fran up in the bow. The Cabin 10 girls were gaining on them.

"Faster, faster!" Ashley shouted from behind, and Darci strained forward, then back, paddling as hard as she could. They were almost flying now. They couldn't let Cabin 10 beat them, they couldn't, they couldn't.

But the water had grown rougher, and cold spray kept flying in Darci's face. Then a gust of wind whipped across them and the canoe lurched to its side and slowed for a moment.

Looking back over her shoulder for an instant, Darci saw the bright green canoes all strung out behind them, rocking like leaves on rough water. Babs, in the motorboat, was busy with one of them, a canoe that was tipped on its side.

Darci straightened, paddling furiously, through the choppy water. Oh, no! Now she saw Bettina's canoe pulling up fast alongside theirs. And there were the two buoys up ahead, and in just a few minutes the race would be over.

Darci flung herself into it, her hands in an iron grip on the paddle. Go, go, she begged herself, and like a miracle the canoe shot forward.

But now what? Bettina, with an angry glance in their direction, her dark hair whipping across her face, was turning her canoe. Darci could see her arms straining to drag hard on her paddle, swinging the canoe this way. And then it knocked into Cabin 13's with a hard bump and pushed them off course.

"Watch out," Darci cried. And she could see it

all, the triumphant look on Bettina's face, the pleased one on Fran's.

But too late, it didn't matter now. It was all too late. Because Bettina's canoe shot ahead of theirs and raced between the buoys and across the finish line. And on the wind the words flew back to them, "We won, we won!"

13. Does He or Doesn't He?

"If I didn't hate the idea of ratting on someone, I'd tell on them." Ashley frowned as she began to stack up plates, rattling the silverware noisily. She and Darci and Julie and Sara were discussing the canoe race again while they cleared the tables in the Mess Hall.

"I know," Darci agreed. "I feel the same way." If only Babs hadn't been busy with the tipped-over canoe. If only someone else had been close enough to see what had really happened.

Just then the door to the Mess Hall opened, and Princess poked her head in, her long, dark braid of hair hanging over her shoulder. "Ah, Sara, there you are. As soon as you're done, can you come over to Arts and Crafts? We want you to make a poster for us."

"Oh, sure." Sara's eyes lit up. "I'd love to." Sara had done several posters for the camp, and everyone liked them. "What's it for?"

Princess wriggled her eyebrows, looking pleased. "Big doings. There's a carnival in Camden, and both camps are going to visit. So hurry over." She whisked out the door, her braid of hair flying out behind her.

The girls looked at one another and began to smile. "A carnival?" they echoed.

"In town with the boys?" Ashley's face went from cross to delighted. "How fabulous. We can go shopping. We can be with Rolf and Greg."

"Fantastic!" Darci exclaimed. "I was afraid I wouldn't see Greg anymore." Of course, there was the hope she could come back to camp next year, but that was far away and not exactly a sure thing.

"Think of all the great rides we can go on," Julie was saying. "I hope they have a Ferris wheel." She grinned from behind the stack of plates she was carrying.

"Yes, and maybe there will be crafts and stuff we can buy at the fair," Sara said.

Soon everyone was talking about seeing the boys and what they could do, and the things they could buy: maple sugar, pine pillows, maple syrup and other gifts to take home. And by noontime Sara had an almost professional-looking poster up on the camp bulletin board. COME TO THE CAMDEN CARNIVAL, it read above pictures of balloons and a Ferris wheel in bright colors.

When Darci and Ashley stopped to admire the poster again after lunch, a crowd of younger girls had gathered. They were admiring a second poster of Sara's, which had been added to the bulletin board. It was a drawing of a brown wooden bird feeder she'd made in Crafts. She'd hung it on a tree branch outside their cabin, and they all enjoyed watching the birds gather to eat the cracker crumbs they put there.

Underneath the poster was a notice urging all the campers to come by and see it.

"Look at that," Darci said proudly. She turned to the crowd. "The bird feeder is really great. Sara built it. You should come and see it."

"She built a birdhouse?" one of the younger girls said. "What a great idea."

Just then Babs appeared in the middle of the clearing and blew her whistle for the start of morning activities. The younger girls all began to move off in different directions. One of them called over her shoulder as she went, "Maybe you guys will win the silver cups."

But then a voice spoke scornfully behind them. "Oh, I wouldn't go that far." It was Fran, with Bettina coming up behind her. "A bird feeder isn't that big a deal." Fran hooked her arm through Bettina's. Both of them wore their leather bracelets, as usual. "Besides, we're going to win. We've been coming here for years, don't forget."

Darci tried not to show that she was worried, though she did wonder from time to time if that gave them a big advantage. "We remember. You've told us before." She shrugged.

"You were lucky you could do that," Ashley said. "But I don't think that'd be a very fair reason for you to win."

"Yes, I hope our cabin has a chance, too," Darci said. Thinking of things being fair made Darci remember the canoe race yesterday.

And Ashley must have had the same thoughts, because to Darci's amazement, she suddenly blurted out, "It wouldn't be fair to win by cheating in a canoe race, either."

There was a terrible silence for a moment, and Bettina's face went cold and stiff. "What are you talking about? We didn't cheat."

"Yeah." Fran jutted out her chin and scowled. "Bettina was doing a great job of steering our canoe. I know she was."

"But your canoe bumped into ours, don't you remember?" Darci said. Typical of Bettina and Fran never to say they were sorry or anything, just to act as if it hadn't happened!

Bettina's green eyes glittered. "It was very windy yesterday, don't *you* remember?" she said nastily.

"I'll never forget," Darci said coolly. And looking at this tall, so-sure-of-herself girl, Darci decided Bettina was lying about the wind, and the canoe race, and the note, too, and even lying to herself.

But before they could say anything more, Babs came hurrying up to them. "Girls, come on. Time for your morning activity."

So there was no more time to talk, but all through the morning Darci kept thinking about Bettina and Fran. And when she and Ashley were swimming later, Darci said to Ashley, "I'm glad we said what we did to Bettina and Fran. They shouldn't get away with that completely."

Ashley made a wry face. "It bugged them, didn't it? But, oh well, who cares?" Ashley flipped back her wet, dark hair and laughed. "Listen, Darci, forget them. We are going to have so much fun when we go into Camden."

"Ashley, you're right." Darci plunged into the water in a big, splashing dive. It was going to be great to go to the carnival and see Greg again. And unless she and Ashley wanted to make a fuss about the canoe race, there wasn't much they could do about it now.

The whole camp was excited about the carnival. That was all everyone talked about for the rest of the day. And Darci kept thinking about Greg and how he must like her. Ever since the camp fire she'd felt that way. Maybe they could go around the fair together. They could talk about all kinds of things, like exchanging addresses and writing to each other next year. She'd find out if he had any plans for coming back next summer.

"Oh, Ashley, I can't wait," she whispered that night when they were getting ready for bed.

"Me, neither, Darci." Ashley looked just as pleased as Darci felt. "I know I'll see Rolf. Maybe the four of us could hang out together, like a double date. Wouldn't that be fun? I'm going to get up really early tomorrow so I have time to put on all my makeup. Do you want to borrow some?"

"Thanks, Ashley. Maybe just a little now that my poison ivy is gone." Darci smiled at Ashley. How could she ever have a more generous friend?

The next morning when Darci woke up, sun was streaming through the cabin windows, and birds were singing outside. Darci lay for a moment, listening, trying to identify the birds from their songs. There was the harsh cry of a crow, the twitter of wrens, perhaps, and wasn't that the bubbly song of the purple finch? Anyway, it was a perfect day for going to a carnival.

"Yoo-hoo, are you awake?" Gail's voice broke the silence. "Time for the gang to get up." Gail had been very pleased with the posters yesterday and kept calling the four girls her winning gang.

Darci flung back her covers and jumped up to get ready for the day.

Right after breakfast they headed for the parking lot, stopping for a minute to look at the bird feeder.

"Hurry, kids," Gail called. By the time they reached the parking lot it was like the first day of camp, with boys and girls milling around everywhere and the buses starting up their engines.

"This way," Babs and Princess called out loudly, trying to get everyone to line up by the buses. Darci and Ashley followed the others and got in line. While they stood there, they both looked eagerly around, Darci hoping to catch a glimpse of tall, blond Greg, and Ashley looking for Rolf.

"Do you see him? I don't see Rolf," Darci whispered to Ashley.

"Move on, girls," Babs called out. Darci and Ashley climbed in the bus and headed for the few remaining vacant seats up front. But before sitting down, Darci scanned the rows of faces, boys and girls, some sitting in pairs, some not. Then Darci had a terrible jolt of surprise. There was Greg. He was already on the bus. And someone on the seat next to him was laughing and talking to him. Bettina!

"Everybody sit down," the driver called impatiently. She looked pointedly at Darci, so Darci turned and plopped into a seat next to Ashley. But she felt numb. What a start for the day at the carnival!

14. Bump, Crash

How did Bettina always get there first? Then Darci had an even worse idea. Maybe it was Greg's idea they sit together. Did that mean Greg liked Bettina after all?

Darci stared miserably out the bus window. Dense green woods and low stone walls bordering open meadows raced past. They drove by a farm with its red barn and white house and cows in a field nearby. Just because Greg sat with Bettina didn't mean this wasn't still a terrific trip, Darci told herself — and didn't believe it.

"Darci." Ashley leaned toward her. "Darci, don't look sad. She probably pushed her way into that seat. You know how she is."

Darci smiled at Ashley. "I wish. But I don't know. They seem to be having a great time." She allowed herself one quick glance over her shoulder but couldn't see Greg and Bettina because they were so far back.

"He's just being polite, I bet." Ashley shook her head, swinging her red earrings. Ashley's face was covered with a layer of thick makeup and bright blusher.

"Ashley, you look really good," Darci said.

"Oh, do I?" Ashley smiled. "I'm going to find Rolf the minute I get off this bus. I know he'll want to walk around with me." Ashley broke off. "Listen, just give Greg a chance. I bet he'll want to be with you, too."

Darci straightened up proudly. "Well, I'm certainly not going to hang around and wait for him to notice me."

She looked out the window again. Still, it was a big disappointment, especially since it was the final week of camp and maybe her last chance to be with him. She'd probably been foolish to be so sure Greg liked her. But after that night at the camp fire, she couldn't help thinking it.

Now the bus was rolling into the little town of Camden, down a main street, past small stores, a hardware store, a market, and two gas stations. Up ahead was the carnival. Darci heard a sudden burst of music and saw a Ferris wheel and a merry-go-round whirling 'round and 'round.

The bus stopped in a dusty parking lot, the other bus pulling alongside. All the boys and girls began to push out of their seats, laughing and talking. Babs stood up and blew her whistle.

"Quiet, people," she shouted in her husky voice. "Please listen. We'll be returning at five o'clock. Meet back here in the parking lot at that time. The camp has arranged for you to enjoy the rides all afternoon. But shopping at the booths will be up to you. One thing . . . *do not leave the carnival area. No walking around town.* Okay, everybody, ready?"

"Yeah-h-h!" The whole busload of the eager campers cheered loudly and began to spill out of the bus, Darci and Ashley among the first. And there in the crowd of kids, Rolf was waiting, waving at Ashley.

"Oh, Darci! I'm sorry. Do you want to come with us?" Ashley was trying to be sympathetic but her eyes beneath her dark bangs were already big and excited.

"Thanks, that's okay, Ashley. I'll go find the others. There they go. Sara, Julie!" Darci called. "Have fun," she told Ashley and dashed off after her other cabinmates. She certainly wasn't going to wait around to see Greg get off the bus with Bettina and maybe go off with her.

When Darci caught up with Sara and Julie, the three of them began to circle the whole carnival, looking at everything. Julie and Sara apparently didn't know about Greg and Bettina sitting together on the bus, and somehow Darci didn't feel like telling them right away. Julie bought a frozen custard cone. Sara lingered at a booth of pictures drawn by local artists, and Darci went to look at them, too. There was one of a covered bridge that made Darci wish she had enough money to buy it for her parents, for their den at home. But another booth offered maple sugar candy in the shape of leaves and pine trees, and Darci decided to come back later and buy that instead. Her brothers would really like it.

As they walked on, Darci sneaked a few glances around the carnival area. There were camp kids everywhere, piling on and off the rides and lined up by the booths. Darci didn't see Greg though, or Bettina. Was Bettina going to get to be with him the whole afternoon?

"Let's go on some of the rides," Julie said.

"Yes, let's," Darci agreed. She looked about quickly. "How about the bumper cars?"

Julie and Sara agreed. The three of them sped off to the bumper cars. The sun was warm overhead, music was playing, and the smell of hot dogs and buttered popcorn drifted on the air.

Darci climbed into a bumper car, determined to have a good time. "Look out!" she called out enthusiastically to her friends.

The motor started, and the cars began to move.

Darci steered hers fast to the right, smash, into Sara's car. They both screamed with laughter. Then she drove to the left and into another camper's car. She liked careening all around, slamming into the other cars. It made her feel better, and she didn't care so much where Greg was.

Now she'd like to get over to the other side of the circle and bump into Julie's car. But someone banged into her from the rear. She tried to turn out of the way but was crashed into again and again. Who was doing this? She threw a hurried glance over her shoulder. It was Greg, grinning at her.

"Hi-i-i, Darci. Gotcha, didn't I?"

"Well, I'll get you," she shouted back. She spun the wheel and hit him good and hard.

"Yow-e-e-e," he laughed. "You got me." He tried to heave his car out of the way, but other cars were crashing all around, getting in the way, and their drivers were laughing and screaming. Somehow Darci managed to turn her car and hit Greg's again. She burst out laughing at his look of surprise. Then he swerved and crashed into her. They were both laughing as the motors stopped.

"All out! Give others a turn," the young man in charge of the bumper cars called.

Darci climbed out and stood, pretending to be

waiting for Sara and Julie. She hoped Bettina wasn't around here, too. At least she didn't see Bettina anywhere. Instead she saw Greg hurrying toward her.

"Darci, wait. What are you going to do now?"

"Well, I haven't decided. I was with my friends." She looked around for them again but didn't see them. She turned back to him. "Maybe I'll go on the Ferris wheel."

"Hey-y-y." He grinned. "Fantastic. I'd like to do that, too. Can I go with you, Darci?"

"Oh, sure," she said, pleased. Suddenly the day really was a terrific day. Everything began to seem like a movie as she and Greg moved through the crowds toward the Ferris wheel, and Darci talked easily with Greg. She wished she could spot Ashley and Rolf so they could all be together just the way they'd planned. Instead she saw Bettina, who scowled at them as if she had a stomachache.

But what Bettina did wasn't important to Darci now. She and Greg were soon sitting side by side on the Ferris wheel as it began to lift slowly around and up in the air. The music was playing loudly, and Greg's hand was pressed right next to hers as they grabbed the bar across the seat.

"Hey, Darci, this was a great idea," he shouted in her ear and she nodded, smiling. This had to mean he liked her, didn't it?

"Look, Greg, you can see the whole world from here." Now they were way up at the top, up so high you could see everything, the woods and fields far away, then closer in, the little village and its main street lined with small shops. But what was that? Darci stared, not believing her eyes. There, hurrying down the street away from the carnival were two kids in green-and-white camp clothes, a tall boy and a girl with a mop of black curly hair. And even from the back they looked just like Ashley and Rolf. But where were they going? Didn't they know they weren't supposed to leave the carnival?

15. The Ferris Wheel

Darci started to worry. As the wheel swung down and then around and up again, she craned her neck, tried to get another look at the main street. But she couldn't see anyone dressed in green-and-white camp clothes there.

Had that really been Ashley walking down the main street with Rolf? If only she could have seen their faces. It had looked like them. Where were they going? Why? Darci felt puzzled. Then she had a more terrible thought. What if someone found out? What if Ashley got in trouble? That would be bad for Ashley, and bad for Cabin 13, too.

All these thoughts buzzed around in her head like a cloud of worried bees.

"Darci, what're you looking at?" Greg leaned toward her and spoke in her ear. The music was pretty deafening.

Darci turned back to Greg guiltily. The Ferris

wheel was swinging them down toward the ground now, anyway. She'd lost her view.

"Oh, uh, nothing much. There was so much to see, you know?" She smiled at him, thought again how cute he was. But she felt as if she had just learned a big secret, one she didn't dare tell. "You can see the woods and the cows and everything," she went on nervously.

"Yeah, it's great, isn't it?" Greg grinned, his white teeth shining in the sunlight. "Hey, we're going up again, Darci."

This time as they swung up in the air, Darci tried to scan all the people down below, hoping to find Ashley among them. She didn't see her, but she did spot Julie and Sara over on the far side of the carnival. Maybe they would know about Ashley. Then Darci had a good idea. Maybe Ashley had been sent on an errand by one of the counselors.

That was such a comforting thought Darci was able to turn back to Greg. "I really like it up here." She smiled at him.

"Yeah," he agreed. "Say, you liked that night at the camp fire, too, didn't you, Darci?"

Oh, help! Was her face turning red? She suddenly remembered how she'd mentioned the full moon and all that. "Yes, oh, uh," she said nervously. "What did you think of my talk about birds?"

"Your what?" He leaned toward her. "Your talk? Oh, yeah, I remember. That was good, too."

The Ferris wheel was beginning to come down now. "Too bad. I guess our ride is about over." Greg looked truly sorry. "It makes you work up an appetite, though." The Ferris wheel came to a stop. "Do you want to go get a hot dog?"

He'd suggested they stay together some more! "Sure, I'd love to," she agreed.

As the climbed out of their seat, Darci remembered about Ashley. She took a quick look around at the crowds, hoping to see her. Maybe, while Greg got his hot dog she could slip over to Julie and Sara and ask them about it.

But at the hot dog stand a bunch of kids came zooming up to them, two boys and a couple of girls and then Bettina. Now Darci knew she didn't want to leave the group, though she kept glancing anxiously around for Ashley. They all bought hot dogs, then started to walk around the carnival in a bunch, stopping at various booths. They threw baseballs at a bell in one booth, then moved on to the booth for throwing darts.

When Greg took his turn he got all three darts in the bull's-eye. The man in the booth handed him his prize, a narrow silver bracelet.

"Yay-y-y," Bettina cheered loudly. "Good for you, Greg. That's *such* a pretty bracelet."

"What're you going to do with it?" one of the boys joked. "Give it to your girlfriend?"

Darci felt a terrible desire sweep over her. If only he'd give it to her. That'd be so fabulous. She'd wear it forever. But Bettina stuck close to him and kept saying, "That's really nice, Greg." He just grinned and stuck it in his pocket.

They began to stroll across the carnival some more, and Darci kept looking around for Ashley. The group stopped at another booth to throw hoops at prizes on a shelf. While they were all crowded around that, Darci spotted Sara and Julie. Now was her chance. She hurried over to them.

"Have you seen Ashley?" she asked in a low voice.

Right then she knew something was the matter. Sara and Julie moved close to her. "Darci, we tried to stop her, but we couldn't."

"Stop her?" Darci stared at them. "Where did she go?"

Sara gestured toward the brick wall behind them. "She went there, with Rolf," she whispered. Her dark eyes behind her glasses looked worried.

Darci looked up at the wall and read the large poster tacked up there:

GYMNASTIC EXHIBITION TODAY
THREE TO FIVE AT THE YWCA

"Oh, no," she exclaimed. Ashley would want to do that. She was so crazy about gymnastics. She turned back to Sara and Julie. "I thought I saw her walking down the street with Rolf," she said in a low voice, "when I was up high in the Ferris wheel." She frowned, looking around. "Let's hope no one else did."

"I think maybe no one saw them leave, but I sure wish they'd come back." Julie frowned. "It could get our cabin in trouble."

"She promised she'd stay just a little while," Sara added. "We tried to talk her out of it. She said it was a terrific chance to see some good gymnasts, and she couldn't miss it, and she'd be back soon anyway." Sara shrugged, but she still looked worried.

Darci groaned, a feeling of annoyance starting up inside her. "This really wasn't a smart thing to do." She glanced at her watch. "There's not that much time, either. It's five after four already." She looked around, remembering Greg. He was still over at the booth with a bigger group than ever. "I have to go, but I'll keep watching for her," she promised her friends.

She hurried back to join Greg but it was hard to enjoy the carnival quite as much now, what with her worry about Ashley, and the way Bettina kept sticking right beside Greg. But at least being with a crowd made it easier to keep an eye out for Ashley and Rolf.

Suddenly, a whistle blew shrilly over the noise of the carnival, and the music stopped. And then there was Babs standing up on a chair by a booth. She had a megaphone, and she shouted into it:

"All right, boys and girls. It's almost time to go over to the buses. Boys will be in bus two, girls in bus three. This is a five-minute warning. No more rides. You can make your last purchases, then get over to the buses."

Everyone started pushing in different directions. Darci felt panicky. Should she go try to find Ashley and Rolf? But no, there really wasn't time. Surely they'd come any minute. She remembered then about the maple sugar, hurried over to the booth, and bought it quickly. She also bought a pine-scented pillow for her dad and mom. She kept glancing up the street but there was no sign of Ashley or Rolf. Why didn't Ashley get back here? How could she do this?

16. "Here"

Darci moved with the crowd over to the bus area, but she kept glancing over her shoulder, hoping to see Ashley and Rolf. The counselors were all busy making everyone get in lines, the girls in one, the boys in the other. What a disappointment not to be able to sit with Greg on the way back. Babs and Princess ran up and down, hustling girls this way and that, blowing their whistles.

Darci hurried over to Julie and Sara. They huddled together and began to discuss Ashley and Rolf. Was Ashley wearing a watch? No one could remember. If they would just come and come now, they could blend in with the crowd. They noticed Bettina and her friends nearby in line, so they lowered their voices.

Suddenly the line up ahead grew quiet. "Listen, everybody," Babs shouted in her husky voice.

"Now we're going to call the roll. Please answer 'here' when I call your name."

Darci and her friends looked at one another in horror. They hadn't expected this. "What'll we do?" they whispered. "Oh, Ashley, come on back here," Darci exclaimed.

But it was too late to do anything, because Babs had started to call out names.

"Sara Abrams," Babs called in a minute. Sara turned around fast and said, "Here."

And so it went, "Here," "here," "here," one after another answered.

"Darci Daniels."

"Here," Darci said mechanically, but her brain was whirling with worry. Was there something she could do, some way to help her friend?

She heard Julie say, "Here," and others up and down the line. Babs was getting close to the T's, close to the name Ashley Thomas. Darci's palms began to feel damp. Suddenly she knew what she could do. But should she? Would it be right? She stared down at the ground, frowning, trying to figure it out.

She heard the names Michelle Puloski, Linda Tamura and then Ashley Thomas. "Here." The word flew out of Darci's mouth almost without her even intending it to. It hadn't been very loud. Still, she had said it.

And Babs went on calling the role and Darci took a deep breath. She raised her head and rolled her eyes at her friends. So they were safe for the moment. If only Ashley and Rolf would show up soon, they might not even be noticed. And if they didn't, if she and Rolf missed the buses, well, it wasn't that far to camp, only about a mile and a half. They could walk it easily.

Darci glanced toward the boys' bus again. The boys were almost all on board now, so maybe they hadn't had a roll call. The girls' bus was still only partly filled, and the line moved slowly forward.

But why did Bettina keep peering back at them? She looked so nosy, too. But wait, what was happening now? There was a stir in the line. Bettina was stepping out, and her friends were calling to her, "Bettina, Bettina, no! Come back." Why? What was going on?

But Bettina just shook her head in a determined way, and she marched up to Babs and began to talk and talk, and Darci saw Gail step closer and listen, too.

The line continued to move forward and now Darci could hear Bettina's words. "She's not here. I know she's not. See?" Bettina flung out her arm toward the line of girls.

Babs looked up from her list with a puzzled

frown. "I called her name. I thought I heard her answer."

Darci froze with fear, but luckily Bettina said, "You must have made a mistake! You can see, she's not here."

Babs and Gail both turned and scanned the long line of girls.

"Listen to her," Darci whispered heatedly to Sara and Julie. "She's ratting on Ashley."

"Oh, she's disgusting! Why can't she keep her mouth shut?" Julie frowned angrily.

"She's really trying to get us in trouble," Sara agreed.

"And she's doing it, too. This is terrible." Darci turned worriedly to survey the carnival area again. Crowds of townspeople were drifting back into it, and the music had started up. Why didn't Ashley come, anyway? Darci didn't know whether she felt more cross with her friend or with that blabbermouth, Bettina.

Suddenly through a group of women and little children, Ashley came running toward them with Rolf right behind her.

"Look, they're back," Darci whispered to her friends. And as they turned to watch, they saw Gail start out to meet them, her face cross in the late afternoon sun.

"If only Bettina had kept quiet, they'd have

been just a little late, that's all." Julie muttered. "Probably no one would've paid any attention."

"Look at Bettina now," Darci said. "Doesn't she look pleased?" She was standing there, smirking and watching the whole scene, plainly loving it.

But the line was moving forward, and now Darci and her friends had reached the bus and had to climb aboard. Sara and Julie took a seat together. Darci took another, saving the empty half for Ashley, though she was so angry with Ashley she almost didn't feel like doing it.

Some younger girls filled the seats in front of her. They were all giggling and talking about the great time they'd had today. Darci wished she felt as happy.

Looking out the window, she saw the boys' bus pull off down the street. Would she ever see Greg again? For a moment that was all she could think about.

In a minute Ashley boarded the bus, too, her worried eyes darting guiltily about. Then she spotted Darci. She followed the others down the aisle and flopped in the seat next to Darci.

"Oh, Darci, I'm sorry." She leaned toward Darci. "I hear that rotten Bettina blabbed on me. One of the kids just told me."

"Yes, she figured out you weren't here," Darci said stiffly.

"Oh, Darci, you're mad, aren't you? I mean mad at me, too." Ashley looked really unhappy. "We meant to get back in plenty of time. I never dreamed they'd call a roll. Darci, I'm really sorry."

"I tried to help you," Darci said. "I answered 'Here' for you when Babs called out your name."

"You did?" Ashley gave her a grateful smile. "Thanks for doing that."

Darci looked out the window briefly as the bus lumbered back down the main street of Camden. She hadn't really liked doing that, the funny feeling it gave her. She turned back to Ashley. "I thought I had to do something, but I don't know if I should've." She frowned, wondering, how much were you supposed to do for a friend?

"Well, thanks anyway, Darci. I know I shouldn't have gone. I just wanted to see those gymnasts so much and Rolf wanted to, too. I figured if I asked Babs she wouldn't let us go."

Ashley looked really sincere and sorry. "I didn't want to get our cabin in trouble, just when we were doing so great and all." She groaned. "And Gail was pretty upset with me, too. Oh, why did I do it?"

Darci looked at Ashley, drooping on the seat there, her eyes sad under her dark mop of hair. Memories of all the good times they'd had together came sweeping over her. And Darci remembered

120

the time Ashley had helped her go into the woods to meet Greg. That hadn't been quite the right thing to do either, had it? Her crossness melted away. "I know, Ashley. Of course you didn't mean to get us in trouble. I was just worrying about those darn trophies. You know." She smiled a little and shrugged. "But being friends is more important."

17. Winners

It was the last day of camp. All the races and swim meets were over, the waterskiing and the games were finished. The day had come to pack up their belongings, board the buses and head toward home. But first the trophies and the awards had to be given out.

The night before it had rained, and that morning at breakfast the air seemed chilly and damp. Darci knew she would be glad to get home again, back to her family and her own room, back to her old friends. But as she looked around at all the faces, she felt a sadness as well. She might never see any of these girls again, her new friends in her cabin, Sara and Julie and Ashley, and these other girls, too.

She wouldn't mind not seeing the Cabin 10 girls though, especially one of them. Looking down the rows of tables in the Mess Hall she noticed something.

"Ashley," she whispered, "Bettina is not with her group again this morning. I've been noticing that lately. She's only with Fran. I wonder why."

Ashley leaned forward to take a look, then turned to Darci. "Maybe Lana and Gillian want to sit with someone else." She giggled. "I don't blame them."

But what had happened with Bettina? Her group had always stuck to her like glue, but lately they didn't seem to be doing that.

That afternoon everyone gathered in the clearing for the final ceremonies. The girls were all dressed in their going-home clothes. They sat in rows of folding chairs while Mrs. Burkett and the counselors stood by a table up front where the silver cups gleamed in the sunlight.

"What do you think our chances are?" Sara leaned forward to whisper to the rest of them.

Darci shrugged. There was no use worrying about it anymore now.

The girl sitting on the other side of Darci, Linda, must have heard. "Most of the kids think Cabin 10 will get it," she said in Darci's ear. "But I wish it would be somebody else, like your cabin."

Darci smiled at her and mouthed "Thanks." Bettina wasn't really so popular, but she *was* admired. Darci wanted to turn around and scan the audience, but now Mrs. Burkett was speaking.

She talked a little about what a great summer it had been, what an outstanding group of girls they were. Darci wondered if she said this every year. Then she began the awards part. Special certificates were given to the younger girls for various things, such as having clean cabins, and being good campers. Then plaques of merit were given to the older girls: best musical talent, Lana; leadership, Bettina. Bettina accepted it with a look that said she thought she deserved it. Michelle and Fran both received one for best volleyball player. Darci wished there would be one for waterskiing. But it was new this year, and there was no award. Sara received one for best artwork. She looked terribly pleased when she went up to get it, while Darci and Ashley cheered loudly for her.

"And now . . ." Mrs. Burkett stepped forward. "Each year we have the privilege of giving these lovely silver cups to the girls whose cabin has contributed the most." She talked on for a minute, but it seemed like forever. Then she said, "And so this year it goes to Cabin 10." Darci felt such disappointment sweep over her, and she realized she'd almost believed that Cabin 13 might win.

Ashley poked her in the ribs and made a sad face, and Darci squeezed Ashley's arm. True, there were lots of others who would have liked to have won, too. And it was true, Bettina and her friends had excelled at many things.

Still, it was very hard to watch and clap for the Cabin 10 girls as they picked up their silver cups. Darci gazed off to the tall, green pines for a moment, wishing she were far away.

Now there was more applause as the Cabin 10 girls headed back to their seats. As Darci watched them, she saw something that surprised her. When Gillian and Lana passed down the aisle, Darci noticed that neither one of them was wearing her friendship bracelet. She craned her neck to see where they were sitting. The Cabin 10 girls weren't sitting together! Fran sat with Bettina, but Gillian and Lana headed for seats way on the other side.

Suddenly, Darci realized that Mrs. Burkett was speaking again, and she turned to listen. Mrs. Burkett was pulling forward a box, opening it, talking about something new this year for the first time.

"It gives me great pleasure," Mrs. Burkett continued, "to give an award this year for the ones who tried the hardest and had good camp spirit, too." She lifted from the box some small silver cups.

And then Darci, to her great astonishment, heard her name, Darci Daniels, then Sara's, Ashley's and Julie's, all of them in Cabin 13!

Somehow, Darci didn't quite know how, she and her friends were all up and moving past the rows of seats and smiling faces, and everyone was clapping for them. And, oh, dream of dreams, now Mrs. Burkett was placing the small silver cup in Darci's outstretched hands, her very own gleaming silver trophy.

18. So Long

Darci and Ashley headed toward the parking lot, where the buses were waiting. They were both loaded down with their gear. Darci had her backpack hooked over her shoulders, her small trophy cosily tucked inside, and her arms were filled with her bag, her duffel, and her tennis racket.

As they reached the scene where all the boys and girls were milling around, climbing on buses and a few getting in cars, Darci looked around anxiously. If only she could see Greg one last time. Was he going home by bus, or was he one of the few going by car? She had to find him, just had to.

Then she happened to notice Lana and Gillian standing right near by. "Ashley, look," she whispered. "Lana and Gillian aren't with Bettina again. And you know what else? They aren't wearing their friendship bracelets, either."

"Huh? That's odd. They always made such a big deal out of those things. Hey, Lana, how come you're not wearing your bracelet?" Ashley called out before Darci could stop her, and she headed toward them.

Darci had to smile a little as she followed Ashley. Ashley always spoke right up about things. "Where's the rest of your group?" Darci asked, coming up to them.

"You mean my sister and Bettina?" Lana asked. Lana was so small and thin, so unlike her sister.

"They're over there." Gillian waved her hand toward the other side of the parking lot.

"We got kind of fed up," Lana said vaguely.

"You did?" Ashley exclaimed. "I mean, I don't blame you, even though you did win the big trophies. But why did you get fed up?"

Gillian looked embarrassed. "We didn't like the way they were doing things," she said simply.

"You didn't?" Darci echoed. How much did Gillian know about the canoe race?

"We didn't think that note was all that funny, either," Lana added. Her thin face flushed a little, and Darci stared.

So they had written it! She wasn't really surprised. Hadn't she known all along?

"We knew you did it," Ashley said drily.

"We didn't really think you'd believe it," Gillian said apologetically.

Darci stood for a moment, not quite seeing the crowd around her, remembering the night she'd found the note. She guessed she had been sort of foolish to believe it, but then, things had really worked out okay. "Oh, well." She shrugged. "That's what really got me started bird-watching."

"Oh — " Gillian said. "Well, you guys did okay this summer. Come on, Lana. Let's go get on the bus."

Even though it wasn't much of a compliment, Darci felt pleased anyway. After the two girls hurried off, she turned to Ashley. "You know, Ashley, thirteen wasn't an unlucky number for us, was it?"

But Ashley was only half-listening. "Oh, right. Look, Darci, there's Rolf. I gotta go catch him. Save me a seat, will you, if you get on first?"

"Sure, Ashley, of course."

After Ashley left, Darci started off to look for Greg. Then she happened to notice a van across the way, with Bettina standing near it. Next to her were two little boys and a tall, dark-haired man and a woman wearing big, white-framed sunglasses. They must be her parents. Bettina was proudly holding up her silver trophy. But nobody was really looking at her or paying attention. Her mother and father were busy picking up the little boys and loading them into the van. Then Fran came rushing up and started hugging Bettina, and then Bettina and her family all climbed into the van, and in a moment it backed up and drove off in a swirl of dust. Lana and Gillian hadn't even been there to wave good-bye to her.

Darci began to push through the crowds again, but she kept thinking about Bettina. It seemed sad that Bettina had lost two friends, sad that her family didn't even seem to care about the trophy that had cost Bettina so much to win. Darci wondered if she thought it was worth it, to lose two friends that way? Did she think a trophy was better than friends? No. It was okay to compete, but not like that.

"Darci," a voice called her. She whirled around to see Greg hurrying toward her.

"Oh, hi," she called out.

"I just wanted to say good-bye." And right there with a thousand people milling past them, he threw his arms around her, around her and all her belongings. Her tennis racket jabbed him in the chest and her duffel bag poked him in the stomach. But he didn't seem to mind. In fact he leaned down, and she guessed what he was going to do. And this time she didn't have any poison ivy to worry about, and somehow she didn't care who was watching. She tipped her face up, and for just a moment she felt his warm lips on hers as they kissed quickly right there in the parking lot.

"Good-bye, Greg." She smiled up at him.

He stepped back, grinning at her. "Listen, Darci, I want to ask you something. Would you be willing to wear this?"

"What, Greg?" A sudden hope started up inside her as she remembered that day at the carnival. He reached in his pocket and pulled out the silver bracelet he'd won there.

"Oh, Greg," she stammered. And even though she was carrying all her gear, she managed to free her arm so he could slip the bracelet onto it.

"Oh Greg! Thank you!" She stared down at it for a minute, surprised and pleased. How good the narrow silver band looked on her tan arm! A feeling of pleasure washed over her. She had wondered what he'd done with it after the carnival, wondered if he might be taking it home to give to someone there. Instead, he must have been saving it all along to give to her.

"Greg, that's really terrific of you!" And looking up at him, she wondered when she would ever see this tall, blond boy again. "How about we write to each other? Do you want to, Greg?"

"You know I do! Let's swap addresses." He dug in his pocket for a pen and a scrap of paper. And now the buses were starting up their engines, and Babs was blowing piercing blasts on her whistle, and Darci knew she would have to go. She carefully tucked the paper he'd given her into her pocket, then looked up at him again. A terrible sadness gripped her.

"Are you going on the bus?" she asked, suddenly hoping.

"No, I have a ride with Mike and his brother." His blue eyes looked regretful. "But I may be back next year. I might be a cabin leader. Will you be coming back next year, too, Darci?"

"I'd like to." She began to back away toward the bus. "I think I'll probably be able to."

"That's great. So long till next year, then," he said.

"Thanks again for the bracelet, Greg." She raised her arm and let the bracelet shine in the sunlight. "I'll never take it off," she promised, and giving him a last smile, she turned to run for the bus, feeling such a mix of happiness and sadness all at the same time.

On the bus, Ashley was waiting for her. "Oh, Ashley," Darci plopped into the seat next to her, puffing with excitement.

"Darci, we're leaving," Ashley wailed. The bus door slammed shut, and the bus began to move slowly down the dirt road, past the green pines and white birches and beyond the lake, shining in the sun.

They both leaned to the window to wave frantically, and Darci caught a glimpse of Greg for the last time. "Ashley, we have to come back next year, don't we?"

"Yes, yes, Darci." They smiled at each other, and Darci knew they would. They'd be in the games and races and maybe even win the big trophies next time! But the best part would be just being here with all her new friends again.

About the Author

MARTHA TOLLES says she wrote about going to summer camp because, "Like Darci, I went to camp in New Hampshire one summer and had some surprising experiences. I also had to learn to deal with competition, something we all must cope with throughout life."

A graduate of Smith College, Mrs. Tolles is the author of *Darci and the Dance Contest, Who's Reading Darci's Diary, Katie's Baby-sitting Job, Katie for President* and *Katie and Those Boys.*

Her books, which have sold nearly two million copies, were inspired by her five sons and one daughter. She and her husband, an attorney, live near Los Angeles.

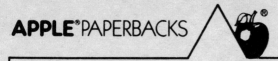